frozen by time

I0679708

Chhavi Kashyap

Woven Words Publishers OPC Pvt. Ltd.

Registered Office:

Vill: Raipur, P.O: Raipur Paschimbar,

Dist: Purba Midnapore, Pin: 721401,

West Bengal, India.

www.wovenwordspublishers.in

Email: editor@wovenwordspublishers.in

First published by Woven Words Publishers OPC Pvt. Ltd., 2018

NOVEL

IMPRINT: WOVEN WORDS LAUNCHPAD

ISBN 13: 978-93-86897-20-6

ISBN 10: 9386897202

Price: $10

Printed and bound in India

ACKNOWLEDGEMENTS

Okay, the acknowledgements part. I don't know why I literally find this part funnier than any other. Oh, how I remember when I was in 7th-8th grade, we were asked to write-acknowledgements, about the author and summary after reading a novel as project work. I never thought I'd be implementing this on practical grounds! We all grow up so fast. Though, this part is the most important ones and people look forward for this part, the most so here it is.

I'd like to thank my parents. I'm blessed to have you both by my side always, from loving me unconditionally to supporting me and motivating me to do more. You guys bring out the best in me! I love you the most.

I always loved writing. I started writing songs from a very young age and then jumped on to writing poems. After getting appreciated for my poetries, I tried to pen down some short stories. I started writing small episodes which I used to update every week, and then I wrote a short story titled-Forget Me Not, and sold eBooks of it. Never have I ever thought in my wildest dreams that I would get such a huge and amazing response to my eBooks. I started working with Ecanus as a core member- a place which provides platform for the writers. I contributed my writings for anthologies. That's when I had decided that it's high time to publish my novel as well. In this journey, I met many people, who inspired me, who filled me with love and appreciated my work and talent. I met people who were senior to me and shared their experiences with me and guided me, and the juniors who motivated me to work harder, since I can be very lazy at times.

Friends who became family, the ones who were there always, thank you for sticking around with me.

After working two years on this novel, I bring you a beautiful romantic story with various twists and turns to leave you breathless, with a hope that you will shower the same amount of love you gave to my Ebook- Forget Me Not, or maybe more!

To my dearest mom and dad. Your darling Chhavi will always love you.

PROLOGUE

It was a dark corridor. She sat on a couch, waiting impatiently. The only light entered was through the transparent window just a few steps ahead of her. It was long and wide. It gave a complete view of all the places nearby. She was alone in the corridor and others were at the places where they needed to be. She didn't care much as she was lost in her own world. She looked outside to turn her attention. The sun was to set. It was a late evening. It created a rose-pink color to the sky. And immediately the sky turned into red, orange, pink and many other colors to notice. There was a little garden. A couple was sitting and enjoying the view. There was a parking lot and she could see people coming inside and going out a*lways chasing lives.*

The nurse called out her name and walked out of the room. The nurse was smiling at her as if she was trying to give her sympathy. The nurse looked at her as if she was a child, who has lost her mother.

The nurse smiled at her and said, "Dear, Doctor's waiting for you."

She shifted her eyes to the nurse's and nodded. She tried to stand with the support of her crutches and, walked with the nurse who led her into the room.

The doctor sat in front of her behind his table. There was a laptop, envelopes on the table. It was quite messed. The doctor looked at her and smiled. She did not return the smile. He kindly asked her to take the seat.

"Bruises on both arms, legs, breasts, broken leg, head injuries. That is a hell lot of injuries. Let me guess, Accident? Was it?" Doctor said.

She looked at him but did not reply. He looked disappointed since she did not speak to him.

"Okay, I'm prescribing you some medicines; it'll help you to get recover with your head injuries. Bruises will heal after some time; I've prescribed some ointments for it. And for your leg, I would suggest a weekly visit, to a physiotherapist."

With the help of her crutches, she stood up. And, she took the prescription from the doctor. These medicines would heal the physical pain but *were there any medicines that would heal the mental pain and, the broken heart? The pain I feel with each and every breath I take?* She wondered.

CHAPTER-1

(Present)

New Delhi. It is the metropolitan city and the capital of India. Here, *people are always in a hurry, always in a rush. They're in a constant rush to achieve more and more, leaving behind their basic needs. They run faster than time. They give in their hundred percent.* But, there are plenty of things in which, people are divided into. Bosses and his employees, employee of the month/week, employee who works hard for promotions, but does not get success, employees who do not work at all, but gets promoted. This was, one of the circles of our lives. The other circles may be the social circles, the student circle, the love circle and the list goes on.

We run and chase things which make us curious. Especially curious about the ones; about which we don't know. But, once you have it, you get bored of it. Again, we repeat this until we grow old and too tired to chase. These, are the circles of life. We love, we regret. We cry, and we smile at the same time. We misinterpret things and expect others to understand us. We speak but do not share what our heart wants. We value time, but not humans. This is the circle of life. Indeed, a harsh one. *People challenge their capabilities and their talent. People drown in their thoughts and that is why they envy looking at someone else's success. People put up a burden on self; they destroy their own dreams to become someone else. In this race between life and time, they lose their identity, their own self. And in this cruel world, that's where her circle begins.*

"Naina Thakur?" The Receptionist announced her name.

She walked to her. The room was big. Little kids wandering around. Perhaps, it was their recess. The walls were faded. They were the combination of white and light pink, on alternative walls. There was a big collage where, there were pictures of students performing different co-curricular activities and enjoying the most of it. A little smile landed on her face when she saw two beautiful little girls, with their completely colored palms posed for the camera with huge grin. There was a showcase made of glass and wood with trophies and medals inside. There was a statue of Swaraswati decorated with flowers, which was kept safe inside a big glass showcase. There was a staircase leading down to the accounts section and the other leading up, to the other official sections.

"Ma'am, you may go now." The Receptionist completed and smiled.

She did not return her smile and, walked straight to the next room where the name plate stated, 'principal's office.'

"Hi, May I come in?" She asked before entering the room.

"Yes, you may." The lady said with a smile.

Naina walked inside.

"Take a seat please." The lady said warmly.

She did what was instructed to her and then she sat on the chair in front of the principal's desk. The desk was arranged and was clean. The name plate read, 'Mrs. Kavita Desai'.

She was a beautiful lady, long hair and was wearing black saree with little heavy makeup.

"Naina Thakur. It's a pleasure to meet you. I'm Kavita Desai, Principal of Maxwell High."

"It's nice meeting you, Ma'am." She said.

"So tell me about yourself?" Principal asked.

"Well, I'm from Dehradun. I recently shifted here, in Delhi. I love children and I believe education is the most essential and prior things which should be passed on. Apart from this, I have interests in music and writing. I like traveling and exploring new places."

"That sounds great. Do you have any previous experience?"

"No." Naina said.

"What makes you choose to work with our school and how did you get to know about the job interview?"

"Your school is one of the most prestigious schools, which makes it obvious that the school must have a friendly teaching faculty and well-disciplined students. And, it would be an honor to serve you the best I can. I came across about the interview from a newspaper advertisement."

"How would you handle, a 3rd grader and a 4th grader who are fighting with each other and you're the class teacher of the 3rd grader child?"

"Well, that's very simple. I'll first stop the fight and calm them. Then I'll try to know the depth behind the argument, and then depend upon the reason behind the argument, I'll talk separately to both of them, and initiate a friendly environment."

"Okay, very well. That's all, Miss.Thakur. I must say you really impressed me. Congratulations, you're hired."

"When do I start?" Naina asked.

"From tomorrow, 7 am to 4 pm."

"Okay. Thank You." Naina said.

"Welcome to Maxwell and, all the best." The principal wished.

Naina nodded and walked out in satisfaction.

It was a long day. She went back to her rented apartment. She had this apartment, all to herself. It was well furnished. She went to the kitchen and cooked food for herself. At dining table, she served food and tried to eat, but she couldn't. It was windy outside. It seemed like it would rain. She went near to the window. It was a huge window, revealing a wider view of outside. She could hear the thunderstorm. *It's sometimes nice to know that, when the clouds can't take the burden anymore, they scream.* It wasn't raining but the wind was harsh and wild. Suddenly, the electricity went off. She was afraid of the dark. She couldn't bear the darkness. She squeezed her eyes and held herself by her arms and told herself to stay strong. She had no idea, when she fell asleep comforting herself the whole night. *In the darkness, in her struggles, all she had was herself.*

The next morning Naina woke up early, as it was her first day at work. She got dressed and took all of the essential things she thought was necessary to carry for her first day and stuffed it inside her black and white polka dot hand bag and also, her tiffin box which she knew wouldn't eat but stuffed it inside as well. Before leaving, she caught a glimpse of herself for the last time in the mirror. She wore a saree, a black and grey colored. Open hair. She wore a bindi on her forehead, and a silver wrist watch, simple and elegant. *But somehow, whatever was reflected back, she was not quite happy with it.* However, she left for the school.

She reached the school at 6:45 am. 15 minutes before the time appointed. She goes inside the school premises, straight to the reception. There was an electric attendance taker, especially installed for the teachers. She placed her thumb and her name appeared on the digital monitor with a 'tick'. Quite impressed by the technology, she walked inside the reception, to the corridor of the school. There were plenty of students who had already arrived. She descended the staircase. There was a stage in front of the reception. And, a digital display board wall mounted on the stage. To the right of the reception, there were senior classrooms of the school (6th to 12th) and to the left, were the junior classrooms of the school (kindergarten classrooms & 1st-5th). There was also a library at the left and 2 computer installed classrooms to the right. Naina walked to the left. She was appointed as a class teacher of 5th- C students and she would teach Math. She went to the 3rd floor of the school. That's where she had her classroom. There were students who were running in the corridor, she passed them. At the end of the corridor, to the left was the staff room. She went inside. There were two other teachers sitting. One of them looked up at her and smiled. Naina smiled back.

The staff room was small. There was a long table with chairs, where the teacher could rest in their free time. There were separate 'locker rooms' where the teachers kept their valuables safely. She went inside towards the locker room and kept her bag.

"Hey, you're new here?" Young lady with spectacles asked and smiled. She had her hair all tied up in a bun. She was wearing a huge earing that hung from her ears and landed exactly on her shoulders, a pink and red saree with one big bindi on her forehead. Looking at her one could say that, she was a strict teacher. But, her smile was beautiful.

"Yes. It's my first day, today." Naina said.

"I'm Esha Verma, I teach English here. What about you?"

"Naina Thakur, I'm here to teach Mathematics."

"I'm 5th-A's class teacher, you?"

"They appointed me for 5th-C."

Suddenly the bell rang.

"Oh, this is the call for us all teachers to go to our respective classes." Esha said and continued," So, I'll see you on the break?"

"Sure." Naina said and smiled.

Naina took the Math book and walked out of the staff room. Her class was in the corner of the floor. She saw the classroom. She was a little nervous. She took a deep breath and reminded herself why she was here. She walked in. All of the students saw her and stood from their respective places. "Good Morning, Ma'am." They all said and greeted Naina in one rhythmic tone. This made Naina smile. She didn't remember when the last time she smiled and was genuine.

"Good morning, children. I'm Naina Thakur, Your new math teacher." Naina said and continued, "Kindly open your books and notebooks."

All the students did what they were instructed as. They all took out their books as well as notebooks. They listened to Naina as she taught them new tricks to solve the questions and the word problems. As told by the principal, the students really were well disciplined. She didn't worry about shouting or scolding any child until they were able to understand their mistake by affection. Later, 15 minutes before the class was to end she asked everyone about themselves. Some told their hobbies as watching TV and playing video games. She laughed and suggested that they were very young and they shouldn't be a couch potato. They all should go out to park and play as much as they love to. She told them about different new games that can be played in the park. After the class ended, every student thanked her for making them teach new things. She smiled, nodded and walked out of the class. She had 2 more classes scheduled after the break. She completed the class and went to have her lunch.

"Naina! Come sit here." Esha waved and smiled.

Naina took her tiffin box and sat next to Esha.

"So how's your first day going?"

"Fine. The students are well disciplined."

"Only the juniors here are disciplined." Saying this, Esha laughed.

15

Naina smiled in returned.

They ate their lunch while Esha introduced Naina to other teachers. They all shared their first-day experience with Naina and asked how her first day has been going this far. They discussed the education system today compared to what it was, before. Naina actively took part in the conversation and shared her views, how *'today education isn't about just learning, it's all about passing with good marks'*. She also confessed that parents today burden their children to come forward with better marks no matter what, even though the child is already doing his best. Other teachers agreed with Naina's views. She made a good first-day impression on both -the teachers and the students.

The bell rang and once again, all the teachers went to their respective classes to teach. Naina also went to teach the remaining classes. She had back to back classes, so she could not rest even for a while. She taught the students continuously after the break. Somehow, teaching children made her happy. The small, funny things they did made her forget the burden, the grief buried deep inside her.

Later, after the school timings were over she went back to the staff room to rest for a while. It was 2 pm and she had to stay 2 more hours. She was tired and exhausted from the long day. But at the same time, was proud that she could manage the classes without any problem. She started reading books, later she closed her eyes, and relaxed.

"I know it's hard for you, living your life without me." A voice said.

"I never wanted this. I never wanted you to go away from me." Naina said. Her eyes filled with tears.

"I'm sorry. I shouldn't have done this. I didn't know things would turn out to be this, wrong."

"I know that you love me. It's not your fault." Naina said, crying.

"I'm sorry, Nidhi. I'm really very sorry."

All of a sudden, Naina saw fire in a bungalow and she looks at her hands. It was red. It was blood. But it wasn't hers.

Nidhi screams and opened her eyes. She was breathed heavily and was sweating.

"Hey! Are you okay? What happened?" Esha came running from her classroom and asked.

"Um. Sorry. I think, I just fell asleep and had a bad dream."

Esha grabs her water bottle from the locker, pours it into the glass and says, "Here, have some water."

"Thanks." Naina said.

She tries to calm herself down, while she drinks water.

"It's almost 4 pm, let's pack things up and get out of here." Esha said, and smiled.

Naina smiled back.

Later, back at home. Naina thought about the dream. She was sitting on the grey colored couch; which were in contrast to maroon walls. She wrapped her arms around her knees, close to her chest and rested her head as she slowly loses herself in her own thoughts of her past. *Memories of past can be as aching as much as it can*

17

bring happiness to one's life. Sometimes, you can never get rid of those thoughts. It just simply haunts you in the darkest of nights, making you feel unwanted and worthless. At the same time, it can make you feel vulnerable, devastated and creates a sense of hollowness inside your mind and heart. Memories are powerful enough, to either make you the most successful person or to make you lose every little thing including your identity and yourself. At this point in her life, Naina was completely lost. Lost, in every single way a person can be. She had a house but not a home. She had no one to call her own. She was breathing but not alive. She was lost.

"Naina" A voice brings her back from her past memories to the present.

She walks towards the door and opens it. It was Kanchan, her neighbor. Kanchan looked fine, with her short hair and cat-eyed spectacles. She was in her late 40s, unmarried and lived alone. Naina and Kanchan first met, when Naina shifted to the new flat. Since Kanchan was very social, she greeted Naina and welcomed her by giving her an expensive white wine bottle, and Belgium chocolates. Kanchan also invited Naina, for dinner a plenty of times, but she denies every time with excuses.

"Naina." Kanchan looked at her with weird expressions.

"Yeah, sorry how are you?" Naina said.

"Are you okay?"

"Yes, why?"

"I knocked your door, tried doorbell. At last, you opened the door after I screamed out your name. And, now I'm asking you something and you're not even listening. Is everything alright, sweetheart?"

"Yeah. I'm sorry. I was just tired been a long day, today. What were you asking, by the way?" Naina asked.

"I ordered Chinese food today, but I don't think I can eat all of it alone. Would you like to join in?" Kanchan asked.

"Kanchan, I don't think I..."

"Please don't say no, I don't like to eat alone. Please." Kanchan requested.

Listening to this, Naina remembers something. She remembers herself, that there was a time in her life when even she couldn't eat anything alone. How she insisted her grand-mother to eat along with her.

"Naina, are you coming?" Kanchan said.

Naina smiled and said, "Yes."

They both walked into Kanchan's flat. The dinner was already arranged on the dining table. She sits on the chair as Kanchan serves her food. They began to eat and talked. Naina told Kanchan about her first day at school. How the students were well disciplined and well behaved, the teachers were all friendly and sweet, that she made a new friend named, Esha.

Kanchan was a pediatrician. She told Naina, how she attended almost eight newborn babies, three 5/6-year-old kids, and a 2-year-old baby. She told how the babies were so adorable and how she always has to resist the temptation to play with them. This was the only similarity between them. They both loved children and, had children related jobs.

They talked about the future that they've planned. Kanchan told Naina, how she has planned to open her own big clinic, where babies can come in all the time and would name it, "Baby's Day Out". Naina laughed. When Kanchan asked about her plans, she remained quiet. She thought to herself, "Future plans?" She had planned her future once which came crashing down and she still is, trying to pick up her every broken piece and trying to move ahead of her life but, what about her future? What will her future look like? Will it be cruel, just like it was before? What will happen?

After lots of talking, Kanchan hugged Naina and asked her to come to her flat anytime or especially at eating hours. They both laughed and exchanged goodbyes. Again, she was back into her flat. She remembered when she was very young, she was afraid of the dark and of being alone and how her dad used to comfort her and used to tell her, 'You are brave from the heart and strong from the mind, my darling.' Today everything has changed but, not her. She still is afraid of the dark and being left alone. *Perhaps everyone is afraid of the dark and scared to be alone in life. Afraid of darkness may vary to person to person. Some may define darkness as the demons inside them provoking them to do things they don't want to; some may define darkness as a phase of their life they would want to get over with, or maybe both. Possibilities are many, but conclusion's the same-that no one wants to be left alone.*

She goes inside and, lies on the bed. She closed her eyes. Winds were howling and there was a thunderstorm outside again. Clouds screamed and she could hear the noise. She tries to sleep but ends up witnessing the morning sunrise with her eyes wide open.

CHAPTER-2

After the long night yesterday, the alarm startled Naina. She couldn't sleep the whole night. She walked out of the bed towards the window. It was a pleasant weather. Although, one can't say that yesterday night it rained. The roads were dry and so were the trees. But the wind was blowing. She made herself a cup of hot coffee. She walked towards the main door and opens it, to find the newspaper. She picks it up and walks inside. She sits on the couch and reads while having her coffee. She still had an hour to get ready for the school.

Before leaving, she looked herself in the mirror. She wore a plain red saree with a black border, a small black bindi and a pair of jhumkas whit her hair open. Around 2 pm after teaching the students, the principal asked everyone to come to her office at 2:15 sharp, for a meeting. Esha and Naina were 5 minutes earlier, which was appreciated by the principal. Later, all the teaching staff arrived at the principal's office at 2:15 pm, as instructed.

"Since the school has reopened after the summer break, and the exams will shortly arrive. I don't want the students to be given a burden. They've been really enjoying the break perhaps, making them irregular at studies. There are consecutive holidays. So, I have decided that we will give our students daily assignments, questions, and homework. This way, they manage to get their mind back on the studies. So, teachers! You have to make assignments, questions for your students. Any doubts?" The principal finally finished and everyone nodded with a disappointed face an agreement.

Esha and Naina returned back to the staffroom.

"I really wanted these holidays without any work. But, thanks to this principal!" Esha said, and sighs.

Naina giggles hearing to Esha's statement and says, "I'll be finishing these assignments today itself, I think you should do that, as well."

"Not really, I can't work at home, and I can't stay late here. Mom gets sick worried if I stay out late." Esha said.

Naina looks at Esha with twinkling eyes. As if, she said something which reminded her of something.

"You're really lucky, you live alone Naina. You don't have people instructing you now and then." Esha said and gave her a faded smile.

"Trust me, Esha. You're luckier to have someone who cares about you." Naina said and sighed.

Esha looked at Naina as if she wanted to ask and know her story, but she turned her face away knowing it wasn't a right time to bug.

"I think it's going to rain. How long will you stay here?" Esha said changing the topic.

"Eh, not long. I have to complete this principal's task first."

"Okay, how many questions will you add to the assignment?"

"Not much, according to what I taught to students, 20 would be enough." Naina said.

"Okay, see you around then!" Esha smiled and left.

Naina started working on the given task and started searching new and appropriate questions which could be added to the assignment. She searched the questions from the NCERT book, NCERT Exemplar and a few guidebooks. At last, she completed the work around 6 pm. It was quite late but at least, she was able to complete the work given to her. She wanted to travel to the locals so that she gets acquainted with her surroundings. She was pleased that she could manage to make an assignment of 20 questions today itself. She smiled in relief and placed the sheets inside the locker. She walked outside the school. And, it started raining. It was her worst nightmare. She did not carry an umbrella which she regretted. And there were no auto-rickshaws to be found. She walked further. Trying to save herself from getting wet in the rain, but it simply wasn't her day. It was getting darker and Naina was getting anxious. She was not well acquainted with the place and she was almost lost. In addition to her anxiety, it was raining and there were no auto-rickshaws.

20 minutes passed and she was still walking under the rain, in the dark, trying to recognize her way back home. She tried to call the only person she knew, Kanchan but only to realize that she was in a no network area. The road was completely empty. It was quite dark, yet visible. She saw a bus stand and decided that she would wait there until the rain stops. She walked to the bus stand. Suddenly, she tripped and fell on the road. She screamed in pain. The road harshly scratched her skin and her right ankle twisted. Blood escaped from the cuts on her elbow. She tried to move her legs but, the pain

ceased her. Nevertheless, she had to move away from the road. She was in the middle of it and any car, from nowhere could hit her. She tries to get up again. All of a sudden, a man gives out his hand to her, in a way to help her. She looks up, raindrops running down her face. His face was not visible. And then, his face brightened up in the thunder light. She swallows a lump.

"Are you okay?" He asked.

His voice sounded comforting, warming. He was completely trying to protect his face from the raindrops by placing his right hand on the forehead while offering the other to her. His clothes were completely wet. His hair shined. Again, his face brightened up in the thunder light and revealed his facial features. Naina couldn't stop gazing. His eyes were twinkling and, raindrops running down from his hair, to his forehead, down to the nose and to his lips. His face faded again and, seemed like he gave her a comforting smile.

"Hey?" He said, reminding her, his presence.

"I… I actually fell down and…" She choked. Even the comforting smiles couldn't help her to feel the ease to talk to him.

"Oh my, are you hurt? Wait, let me see." He said and kneels on one leg, stretches his hand to grab her hand and he notices her facial expressions. She was scared. He smiled.

"May I?" He smiled and asked, before he touched her hand.

They were close to each other, so close that she could smell his perfume. She looked at him, into his deep twinkling and innocent eyes. She was mesmerized. *How*

25

can someone look this beautiful? She thought. She realized that he was waiting for her to react; she slightly tilted her head towards her shoulders. And he smiled at her and he nodded. Maybe he took it as a signal of yes. He grabbed her elbow and saw she was bleeding a lot and the blood was flowing continuously.

He looks at her, again, into her eyes. He was concerned now.

"You're bleeding and your skin feels hot. I think you have fever." He said, looking at her.

"I feel fine." She said in a low voice.

"Okay, let's get you under the shade first." Saying this, he signaled at the bus stand and then looked back at her. He still was holding her by her arms and that was giving her chills. He was a complete stranger and she had no idea of what she should do. They were completely alone, in the dark, under the rain, on the road.

He held her by her arms and slowly helps her get up. He tries to get her up back on her feet again.

"Argh." She screams out. As soon as she screams, she grabs his shoulders with her hands and almost falls on him. She was now standing almost hugged to him. She took a deep breath of anxiety to smell the familiar perfume, *his* perfume again. She tries to step back a little, but the pain was unbearable. She squeezes her eyes in the pain.

"I think your ankles are hurt." He said, looking at her, smiling. *Eh, you think?* She thought to herself.

He took his hand and placed it on her back and the other hand, down her waist as he lifted her. As soon as he touched her, she gasps. A sort of electricity flows inside her veins. He held her tightly and walked towards the stand.

They reached the bus stand and he helped her to sit on one of the seats. The seats were silver colored and, were cold. The rain did not stop. He again kneeled on one leg. He looked at her as if asking a permission to touch her. She blinks and again unknowingly tilts her head. He takes it as a yes and, gently holds her feet.

"Argh!" She screams.

"I'm sorry." He apologizes.

He looks at her and she was already gazing at him. He catches her staring, and smiles. She blinks. In this complete silence, in the presence of wind and the sound of raindrops and, the smell of wet soil; Small gestures were exchanged which were more than words.

"I think your ankle twisted when you fell down." He said, looking into her deep black eyes.

You think? She thought again.

"By the way, I'm Vivaan. And, you?" He says and smiles as he gets up and sits on the seat beside her.

"Naina." She says in a low voice.

"Okay. So Naina, we'll drop you safely to your house. May I know where you live?" He says in a soothing voice.

Before she could say anything, she felt as if the place lacked in oxygen and she couldn't breathe. Her head was spinning all of a sudden. Before she could react she fainted and, she would fall on the ground but he grabbed her to prevent her from falling. He gently shakes her, repeating the sentences and questions on loop, 'Naina! Naina! Are you okay? Naina, can you hear me? Oh my god, she has a high fever. I don't even know where she lives'. He expected Naina to come back, to her conscience to answer all his questions but, alas they all went in vain.

He looked at her, her hair strands escaped and fell in between the cavity of her left eyes, down to her lips. Her face was completely wet yet her face was warm and her lips, as well as her cheeks, were baby pink. She looked beautiful. He could simply stare at her, forever. She was a human figure of the definition of 'beautiful'. He distracted himself with her overwhelming beauty and made himself land on the reality that he needs to help her. He picked her up, in his arms, walked down to his car and laid her in the backseat. He was very close to her. He gazed at her and thought, 'How can anyone look this beautiful?' She smelled of strawberries. He smiled. He scolded himself for being so engrossed in his thoughts. He distracted himself and closed the door. He ran towards the driving seat and drove to his house. From the rearview, he kept on checking on Naina in intervals.

CHAPTER-3

It was the time of the dawn and, the rain had finally stopped. Birds were chirping outside and the weather was cold and moist yet, pleasant. The wind was still blowing which caressed the trees gently, and a few dried yellow leaves fell on the ground. It was still cloudy outside. On the inside, Naina was laying on the bed. The room was large. The walls were blue in color. It was a double bed with wooden work with side tables on both sides. There was a flat screen TV in the front. To the left, was sliding windows completely made of glass, from where the sunlight gently brightened up the dark room. To her right, there were a wooden cupboard, mirror and dressing table.

Naina gently opened her eyes, blinked. Her head was spinning and her body felt weak and feeble. She was struck with a sense of horror when she looks up at the ceiling, then moves her head right to left, only to realize that she was in an unknown place, on a bed. She gasps a huge amount of oxygen and tries to move her body. Alas, her body refused to work with her and as a result, she couldn't move from the bed. Her body felt burning hot and her ankle was giving her an unbearable amount of pain when she tried to move her feet.

A woman walked into the room. She looked at Naina and smiled in an apologetic way.

"I'm really sorry mam, I forgot about the curtains." The woman said, rushing towards the curtains and draws them back, blocking the sunlight behind it.

Naina gives the woman an intense and puzzled look.

"I've been asked to take care of you, until sir return. Do you need anything?" She asked in a very polite manner.

"How did I come here?" Naina asked, in a low and husky voice.

The woman gives her, a completely blank look.

"Can I have a glass of water?" Naina asked.

The lady returned the smile, nodded and left.

Where am I? Whose house is this? She thought to herself.

She again tried to get up. But, it just wasn't her day, *again.*

A minute later, a man entered the room. He was holding a glass of water, and a small bowl of tablets. Naina looked at him, their eyes met. She realized that she remembered him. He was the guy from last night. The guy who helped her and also who scared the hell out of her. Her brain reminded her how he was so close to her a night ago. She flushed scarlet at that thought.

They couldn't stop gazing at each other. Breaking the spell, Vivaan blushed to the ground and walked towards her and sat in front of her, on the bed.

"Hi. How are you feeling?" He said, and smiled.

It was the second time Naina was looking at him but it seemed like for the first time. It was dark and rainy, so she couldn't see much of his features. He had straight hairs, in the front and the sides were trimmed perhaps the latest hairstyle. But, it suited him. He had beautiful black eyes. It was simply obvious he was so gorgeous and girls out there would kill for his one look. And his smile, it made him look irresistible. He had full lips with a few pimples on his face. Those pimples and the scars only enhanced his beautiful face.

"Why am I here? What happened?" She asked in a numb voice.

Vivaan frowned.

"Yesterday, you fainted since you have had a high fever. I didn't know your address, and I couldn't leave you alone as well. So, I brought you here." He said.

Naina was still looking at him, observing the way he was speaking, his expressions and gestures. She did not respond. She was embarrassed to be a burden on a complete stranger.

"Don't worry, it's okay, your safety was my responsibility." He said looking into her eyes as if all the words were coming out from his heart.

Naina's eyes widened. *How did he know what I was thinking?* She thought to herself.

Vivaan grinned at her expression. "Here, take them." He says and gave her a glass of water and medicines.

She looked at him, blinked. He smiled at her and said, "Don't worry I'm not a criminal and you really are safe."

She grabbed the glass and took the medicines and as soon as their hands touched, she felt the same electricity flowing through her body. She was completely unknown to these feelings, they were foreign to her neither she wanted to know them so she diverted her mind.

"Thank you, Vivaan. I'm grateful to you that you helped me. But, I think I should be going." Naina said in a hollow voice. It was the first time she said so much after she met Vivaan. She had to put in a lot of courage to speak two sentences properly.

"I can't let you go. You're not okay. You have a high fever and you can barely walk."

"Thank you for your concerns but, I really think I should go."

"Naina, I..." He choked.

"Please. I must leave." Naina requested.

There was something in Naina, a charm maybe. Vivaan couldn't stop looking into her dark and intense black eyes. For the first time in his entire life, he wasn't able to figure out a woman. She was a complete mystery. As if, she was hiding a million things in her eyes, which attracted Vivaan the most.

"Okay. But, I helped you out so much. Wouldn't you reward me with something?" Vivaan said and grinned.

"What?" Naina instantly replied being defensive.

"I'm mean, a reward."

"What do you want?" She asked in a low voice. *Does he want money? Why does he want money? Since it looks like he has a lot of them! What does he want from me then?* She thought.

"I'd like to have lunch with you, here, with me." He said politely, not forgetting to give his million dollar smile.

"Vivaan, I…" She choked.

"It's a request. Please." Vivaan requested in an ultra-attractive voice.

She lifted her eyebrows.

"From the one who saved you from a terrible day, yesterday?" He said in a way as if he's completing his above sentence.

"Okay, I'll stay." She said.

He had no clue as to why, when Naina said I'll stay it practically gave him an unknown reason for happiness. Strange but, it did make him smile and, made him feel more than a feeling of happiness.

"Thank you." He said and smiled at her. She nodded in sense of agreement.

"I think you should sleep now, these medicines would help to reduce your body temperature and the fever effects. I'll take my leave now." He smiled again and before she could say anything, he walked out of the room.

As soon as he left, Naina laid back on the bed. *I have no idea why on earth I'm listening to him. He helped me. I spent the whole night in a stranger's house. Kind enough of him but, I think I should just leave.* She thought. She tries to move her body and again, she felt the unbearable pain in her ankle and, her body refused to work with her brain. *'Maybe that's why he asked you to stay!'* Her conscience said.

Someone opened the door; she shifted her attention and put the conversation on hold. She turned her head in the direction of the door. It was Vivaan, again. This time, he was here with a white colored ceramic bowl. She narrowed her eyes and observed him. A lady came in as well. She was tall, her heavy brown hair carefully pinned into a bun. She wore a black pencil skirt and a white shirt tucked inside. Must be another of his maids Naina thought to herself. The lady took the bowl from Vivaan's hand, and she flushed. Naina watched them carefully and lifted her eyebrows. Eh, The Vivaan effects getting high on the lady, Naina thought and pouted. Vivaan looked at Naina, smiled and nodded. Unable to understand what was exactly going on, she lifts her eyebrows and opens her mouth to speak but, before she could even ask anything, He left. The lady walked towards Naina's side of the bed. Sat on the edge and revealed Naina's feet underneath the sheets.

"Um… What are you doing?" Naina asked, in a confident way than ever.

"Eh, massaging?" Lady said as if she was already irritated.

Naina gives her a completely blank look. The lady looks at her and pressed her lips inwards.

"I've been asked to come this early, to give you a foot massage. I already am tired, so let's not make it more complicated. Shall we?" The lady said.

Eh, she's so damn arrogant. What's her deal? Naina thought.

"I want to talk to Vivaan first." She said kindly.

The lady sighs deeply. She placed the bowl on the side table and walked outside.

Why is he doing all these things? Have I asked him to do all this for me? Why can't he just leave me on my own? Did he help me last night? Fine! This doesn't give him rights, to do all these things. Urghhh. Why can't he just let it go? Naina thought.

She came inside, without Vivaan. Naina lifted her eyebrows and looked at the lady.

"I couldn't find him." She said.

Naina didn't say anything. *What should I do now?* Naina thought.

"Look, if you don't want to do this, I can leave but, money wouldn't be refunded." Lady said.

God! Where have I got myself stuck? Naina thought.

"You still want to do it?" She said raising her voice a little.

Fine, I'll just pay him back the amount. Naina thought.

Naina nodded in approval. Lady sighed deeply. Naina rolled her eyes at her. She closed her eyes as the lady rubbed some oil in her hands and started massaging her feet. *Mmh... Well, it does feel good.* Naina thought. She had no idea when she fell asleep.

CHAPTER-4

Naina heard some noises and she opened her eyes. She yawned. She tucked the hair strands behind her ears which were falling on her face. She rubbed her eyes. She felt far much better than she felt before. She moved her feet a little, and it did not hurt as much as it was hurting before. She sighed and smiled. *Wow, maybe I reacted a lot. I should just thank him*, she thought to herself. She removed the sheets and walked out of the bed. She noticed her injured feet were completely hidden under white dressing. She blinked. She walked further. It was a stinging pain when she walked. But, the pain was somehow bearable. She walked further, and suddenly she stopped. She saw her reflection in the mirror. She was shocked. She was supposed to be wearing a saree but she was wearing a silk black nightgown. She frowned and panicked.

Then, a lady came inside. She saw Naina standing. Naina recognized her. She was the lady from the morning who apologized her for leaving the curtains open. She was carrying a bag in her hand.

"Ma'am, these are for you to wear for the lunch." She said and smiled.

Naina blinked and pouted.

"Your clothes are in the laundry machine at the moment." She said.

Naina lifted her eyebrows.

"When sir came yesterday night with you, he asked me to help you to change into some dry clothes." She said and smiled.

"Oh." Naina said and flushed. Her words comforted Naina. She sensed the fear in Naina's eyes and smiled at her.

"Vivaan sir is a nice man. You don't have to worry." She said and smiled.

Unusual for Naina, she returned her smile.

"You may wear these clothes and when you're dressed, you can come for the lunch."

Naina nodded and took the bag from her hand and carefully, walked into the bathroom. She would have said a no to the clothes but, she could not walk outside the room wearing a nightgown. So, she accepted the clothes readily.

She walked outside the bathroom a few minute later. She wore a beautiful peach colored kurta with golden polka dots on it. And, a neon green salwaar with open straight hair. It was simple yet, beautiful. When she looked herself in the mirror, she was consumed by the bad memories. She stares herself deeply. A few teardrops escape her eyes and roll down her cheek. She sighs. She suddenly heard some noises outside her room. She quickly wipes her tears from the palm of her hands and helps herself with a glass of water. Then, she walks out of the room.

The hall was huge, crème color wallpaper. There was the drawing room after few steps ahead, and then at the left, there was a huge dining table with classy chairs. And a silver chandelier just above the dining table. The table was arranged with plates and glasses. There was a wide glass window behind the dining table.

"I don't understand Mr. Irwin. What is the matter with them? No, I perfectly understand but…. No, I don't want to listen to any of your excuses. It's either you deliver the medicines till 6 pm today, else I have to look for someone else."

Naina saw a lady talking on the phone, she was quite disappointed. She looks at Naina, and she smiles. Naina smiles back. She was wearing black jeans and skin colored formal shirt. She had a grey hair, which she flaunted gracefully in her half-open hair and the other half, tied. She was old but looked a little younger than her age.

"I don't want any further conversation. Thank you." And, she disconnects the phone and walks towards Naina.

"How are you, dear?" She speaks in a very firm and caring voice.

"I'm good. Thank you very much." Naina said in a low voice.

"I'm Dr. Savita Juneja. I'm Vivaan's mother." She said and smiled.

"I'm Naina Thakur. Thank you, for everything." Naina said and flushed.

"Oh, don't thank me! Your safety was our responsibility." She said and smiled.

I didn't know people like her and Vivaan still exist. Naina thought to herself.

Naina smiles at her. She was speechless.

"Why don't we both sit, till Vivaan comes? Come!" She says and smiles. She leads her to the dining table and Naina follows. Savita sits on the main and front chair while Naina on the chair sits beside her.

"So Naina, what do you do?" She asks politely.

"I'm a Math teacher at Maxwell High." Naina answered.

"Oh? You look quite young, though. Have you worked before?"

Naina's brain stops responding and her heart stopped beating. She was forced to go back into the memories of her past, which she was running from.

Then suddenly, Vivaan comes and thankfully the question could finally be left unanswered.

"Hi, mom!" Vivaan grins.

He walked towards the dining table and saw Naina, sitting beside his mother. He looked at her. Her hair open, falling down to her waist. And, carefully a few of her hair strands were tucked behind her ears. She looked nervous, but she looked adorable. She was the epitome of beauty. He couldn't stop staring at her. Naina looked up, and their eyes met. Naina felt the same chills in her stomach as she felt before. Remembering of Savita's presence as well, Naina forced herself to look somewhere else and she flushed. The temperature in the room felt as if it was going down. And Naina felt numb. Vivaan hops into the chair, in front of Naina.

"How are you, now?" Vivaan asked, looking into her deep, black eyes.

Naina flushed again, but she managed to speak up and said, "Better."

"You don't have the fever now, I suppose?"

"No." Naina said in a low voice.

"What about the pain in your feet?" Vivaan asked.

"Bearable."

Vivaan smiled at her and nodded.

"Scarlett, please bring the food to the table." Savita said in a low yet, high pitch.

Listening to this, a young lady whom Naina remembered from the morning and the one who gave her the dry clothes she arrived. She looked at Naina. Naina smiled, and she smiled back. She brought a trolley, in which different bowels were kept. She carefully picked them up and placed on the table. She placed all the bowels, she left.

"Let's start?" Savita said and smiled.

Everyone helped themselves with the food, so did Naina. Later, Vanilla ice cream with chocolate brownie dipped in chocolate syrup was served.

"Thank you, for everything." Naina said, looking at Vivaan and his mother after finishing her dessert.

Everyone was in the drawing room, talking to each other.

"It was our responsibility, dear." Savita said and smiled.

Naina nodded and smiled back, "I think, I should get going now."

"Oh? Are you sure that you can't stay any longer?" Savita asked.

Vivaan looked at Naina just like a small child looks at his father so that he can get himself a candy. Naina purposely didn't look at him, as she knew she wouldn't stop staring and she might say a 'Yes, I can stay' but she didn't want to take any risk for the same.

Why do I want to stay anyway? Naina thought to herself.

Suddenly, before Naina could say anything, Vivaan's phone buzzed. He got up, smiled, "Excuse me." He said and left. As soon as he left, Savita shifted her eyes back to Naina expecting her to answer her previous question.

"I'd really love to stay, but I really can't. But I'll see you soon." Naina said and smiled, tried hard to sound confident in her second sentence. But the truth was that she didn't want to meet them again. She didn't want to meet *him* again. There was something in him, some sort of a magic that Naina was always spell bounded around him or maybe a connection? No matter what it was, she couldn't breathe around him and, she was left awestruck whenever she looked at him. She didn't like such feelings intruding her mind and heart. These feelings had no place in her life, at all.

Savita nodded. And, she called her maid, and she came in the drawing room. She asked her to hand over Naina's clothes to her. And, she goes inside to collect them. Naina herself follows the maid.

Frozen by Time | Chhavi Kashyap

She gave her clothes in a bag. Naina walked to that room where she stayed the night, to collect her phone. She realized she should call Kanchan; she must be very worried since it was only Kanchan who actually cared about Naina, or maybe not only one- anymore. But, her phone was dead. She heard some noises. She walked out of her room. It was Vivaan.

Obviously, who else could it be? Naina thought to herself. He was still talking on the phone.

"No, I don't... Listen, I... I'm sorry, but... Baby, I want to... Yes, I know... No, no I..." Vivaan kept on speaking incomplete sentences.

Naina lifted her eyebrows. Girlfriend, wasn't it obvious? Naina frowned with her thoughts. Vivaan looks at her and squeezed his lips inwards. Naina lifted her eyebrows again. Vivaan smiled. *Why is he smiling at me like that?* Naina frowned.

"Listen, I'll just talk to you later." Saying this, Vivaan hung up and looked at Naina.

"I actually..." Naina said and froze.

Vivaan looked at her and smiled, waiting for her to complete.

"My phone's battery is dead and I had to make a call." Naina completed.

Vivaan walked towards her and, hands over his phone.

She found out the dialer and, there was call history. The top and recent one displayed the name Sharara. *Girlfriend, obviously!* Naina thought. The second one displayed home. She stared at it. *Those four letter word home. It's so ironical that we don't value little things in our life. How we take them for granted. We realize their importance when we don't have them in our life anymore. Just like this small four letter word, home. It's just a small thing, a small word. But, it basically provides us shelter. Provide us a place, where we can hide. Honestly, home is complete when there is someone, waiting for you inside when someone is looking forward to seeing you again- when someone is really worried, when you're not back on time.* But in Naina's case, her home could never be complete.

"Everything's okay?" Vivaan asked.

Naina comes back into reality. "Yes." She said and dials Kanchan's number. Kanchan picks up on the first ring.

"Hello?" Kanchan said.

"Hey, it's me, Naina."

"Where the hell were you? I was so worried about you!"

Naina smiled realizing maybe someone really does care about her after all. "I'm sorry, my phone's battery died." She said.

"Okay, but are you alright? And, where are you?" Kanchan asked.

"I'm okay and, I'm alright."

"Where are you?"

"Umm... I'll explain later."

"Okay, so I'll come to your apartment at 6 pm for dinner okay?" Kanchan said.

"Okay." Naina agreed.

"Take care."

"Yes."

After this, she ended the call and handed the phone to Vivaan. Their hands touched. And again, she could feel the same, knots in her stomach and the electricity in her skin.

What is happening to me? Naina thought to herself. Vivaan smiled as if he knew what she was thinking.

"I'll drop you at your apartment." Vivaan said.

"No, I'll be okay by myself." Naina said in a low voice.

"No, you're not in a condition to walk properly. You still are sick. Please." Vivaan requested.

"Okay." Naina agreed.

Naina and Vivaan walked out of the house, after hugging Savita and exchanging goodbyes with a promise to visit again. Savita forced her to take a few medicines with her, for her well-being and Naina thanking her for her love and care. Vivaan and Naina walked to the car and she told him her address, which he knew where it was located.

"So, Naina I was thinking. Would you like to grab a cup of coffee with me, sometime?" Vivaan asked in a low voice.

Naina lifted her eyebrows.

"Umm… I'd love to but, I have some school assignments to make. So…" She said in denial.

"Oh… that sounds perfect. I'll come to your apartment for the coffee and, I can help you with the assignments and keep a check on your health as well." Vivaan said and smiled.

What? What Just happened? Naina thought.

"So tomorrow at 5 pm?" Vivaan asked.

Naina rolled her eyes. "Umm…"

"It's okay if you're really busy. I don't want to force you." He said kindly.

He helped me so much, plus, it's just a coffee. Naina thought.

"Okay. 5 pm, tomorrow." Naina said and blinked her eyes.

Vivaan smiled in return. "Perfect." He said.

Later, they reached Naina's apartment. And, she walked out of the car. Vivaan came out of the car as well.

"Tomorrow, 5 pm" Vivaan said and smiled.

Naina nodded and returned his smile.

CHAPTER-5

"I was worried about you Naina. Where were you?" Kanchan asked.

Naina narrated the whole incident, to Kanchan without missing out on any detail, about how she met Vivaan last night, on the empty road and he helped her. Kanchan listened to Naina with a lot of enthusiasm and interest.

"Wait, are you saying that you met Vivaan Juneja?" Kanchan asked.

"Yes, I think because his mother is Savita *Juneja*."

"Do you know who they are?" Kanchan asked.

"No."

"Savita Juneja, she's a very well-known pediatrician of Delhi and her son Vivaan, his name comes under top ten lawyers of India." Kanchan completed.

"Like mother, like son." Naina said in a low voice

"They're like really rich." Kanchan said.

"Oh?"

"Yes. It's weird that they treated you so well."

"Weird? Why?" Naina asked.

"That's because generally rich people don't do that!" Kanchan said.

"I know, but he was really nice." Naina said, slowly getting lost in her world.

"*He?*" Kanchan held her hand and pulled her to the reality.

"I mean, Vivaan and his mother." Naina explained herself.

"Is there something?"

"Something as in?"

"You know…" Kanchan gave her a wicked look.

"No, I don't." Naina clarified.

"Anyway, the way you met him? It sounds so romantic! I still am waiting for this to happen to me." Kanchan said.

Naina lifted her eyebrows.

"So when are you going to meet him?" Kanchan asked and gave her a wicked smile.

"Tomorrow 5 pm."

"Nice. Like a date, date?" Kanchan continues to smile.

"No. Like a 'thanks for helping me yesterday and not turning out to be a creep' date." Naina said in a low voice.

"At least, it's a date!" Kanchan laughed.

"Oh, you know what I meant." Naina said.

"No. Not really." Kanchan laughed and lied.

"It's not a date. It's just I'm meeting him because he helped me and I want to thank him."

"Really?"

"Yes."

"That's all?" Kanchan said, concentrating on her expressions.

"Yes." Naina rolled her eyes at her.

"So, you don't feel anything for that guy, with whom you spent hours under the First Monsoon Rain?"

"No." Naina took a second to reply.

"You don't feel anything for that guy who helped you so much?"

"No."

"You don't feel anything for that extremely hot and sexy guy?" Kanchan said, concentrating on her expressions again.

Naina blinks and she was forced to a flashback of Vivaan's beautiful black eyes and million dollar smile, Naina smiled in her thoughts.

"I got my answers." Kanchan said and laughed.

"What?" Naina asked after getting interrupted by Kanchan's laugh.

"Nothing!" Kanchan said and gave her a wicked wink.

Naina lifted her eyebrows.

"Naina, I was really worried about you." Kanchan said.

Naina listened to the words carefully as Kanchan said that sentence. They echoed in her mind till they faded. Someone was worried about her, after all. And, for the first time after so many years, she cried in front of someone.

"Hey..." Kanchan grabs her and hugs her tight to her chest. "What's wrong, Naina?" She asked.

Naina couldn't stop crying. Those tears were falling continuously down to her cheeks and she felt so weak that she couldn't speak. Somehow she managed, and said, "I... I... I feel so happy that... that someone is he...here for me."

"Aw, honey." Kanchan holds her tighter. "I'm here for you." She completed.

She cried for 10 to 15 minutes and Kanchan didn't complain about it or didn't run away from holding her and comforting her.

"Naina, I know the best friend forever concept was better when we were kids, but I want you to know that I'll be your sister you never had. Okay? I'll be there for you whenever you want a person to hold you when you cry. I'll never let you feel alone because you are not." Kanchan said.

This made Naina cried a little more before Kanchan pulled her away, wiped her tears and smiled, "I'm here. Okay?"

Naina smiled.

Being a kid means you have no responsibility. One can do anything, or say anything. Small kids say things; do things, makes promises, which they aren't fully aware of how important they can be, in someone's life. Kids do not take liability for anything they do or say only because they aren't completely aware of their actions. Once one grows up, he's suddenly in charge of anything he says or he does. He's responsible for his own actions or his own words. Promises suddenly are important, because one thinks he'll sustain on his words. But, would he? Alas, no one generally does.

Kanchan pulled her away from her and wiped her tears. "Let's find you something to wear on your date." Kanchan smiled.

"It's not a date!" Naina said hitting Kanchan on her arm.

"Ow!" Kanchan screamed and Naina giggled.

"What will you wear then? A saree?" Kanchan asked in a sarcastic way.

She's right, I cannot wear a saree. But, I only have sarees. What should I do, now? Naina thought to herself.

"Don't worry, I'm here. " Kanchan said as if she was reading whatever was going on her mind and she smiled.

Naina looked at her like a 5-year-old child with twinkling eyes.

"Meet me an hour before you go and meet him, Okay?" Kanchan said.

"Okay." Naina said.

"Okay, now help me with some food. I'm starving and I can't eat alone."

"Sure."

"Chinese?"

"Again?" Naina giggled.

Kanchan giggled, "Okay let's have some Pizza!"

Naina smiled.

Later, she came back to her apartment, after she hugged Kanchan goodbye. She walked inside. It was completely dark. She walked to her bedroom. She caught a glimpse of her in the mirror. Her hair was open and a few strands were falling on her face. She tucked it behind her ears. She looked in the mirror and concentrated on the reflection. She narrowed her eyes and then, she notices a bruise on her neck, which was hidden behind the hair but a little visible. She sighs heavily. She walked into the bathroom and removed her clothes and hanged them. She ties her hair in a bun. It was dark, but not completely. There was faint light which escaped from the curtained window, which lit up the room a little. There was a 6 feet mirror in front of her. She slowly builds up courage and, she looks up, in the mirror. She tried to see herself in the mirror but all she could see that, her body was covered in bruises and scars. She had bruises on her right leg, up to thighs, a scar on her left leg. She had bruises on her both breasts which were hidden under her peach-colored bra, down to her stomach. Few bruises were healing but few didn't as they were deep. Tears cascaded down her cheeks once again as she remembers the haunting and horrifying memories. But she tries to suppress them. She falls to the ground as she couldn't stay strong. As she fell to the ground, her bruised body and her ankle ached hard and she screamed in pain. But, her heart ached more. *The worst kind of pain is when one cannot express it in* words but just feel it in your chest, reminding each and every second you breathe that it exists.

CHAPTER-6

"I think this looks best on you." Kanchan said, looking at Naina.

Naina and Kanchan were in Kanchan's apartment, in her bedroom. The room was really well designed; the walls were dark pink in color and, had her pictures hanging. There was an iron bed, with a flat-screen TV in front of the wall and a dark brown wooden cabinet below it. The wardrobe was of the same color to the cabinet and, to the right of the bed was the balcony which could be entered by a sliding transparent door. There was a 6" inches mirror to the left of the bed. Naina was standing in front of it, staring at her own reflection. Her hair was falling free as usual, and she wore a purple maxi dress, which belonged to Kanchan.

"I don't know why we're even doing this, Kanchan. I mean just give me anything and I'll wear it." Naina said and rolled her eyes at Kanchan.

"Can you wear a short dress? Please?" Kanchan narrowed her eyes and squeezed her lips inwardly.

"No." Naina said.

"Okay, this looks good on you!" Kanchan said and grinned.

"No dresses." Naina said in a low voice, looked at her and lifted her eyebrows.

"What do you want to wear, specifically?" Kanchan gave her an annoying look.

"Kurta-salwaar maybe?" Naina said.

"Okay, I have one. Give me a second." Kanchan said.

Naina shifted her eyes to the mirror and glancing herself at every angle. She looked beautiful. The purple maxi dress did look so fine on her.

"There you go!" Kanchan said and she handed over the clothes to her, "Go change. It's almost 4:30 pm." She completed.

Naina walked into the bathroom. After a while when she came out, Kanchan looked at her and couldn't stop staring. She looked more beautiful than she looked before. She wore a white full sleeve lace kurta and a black salwaar. Kanchan was left awestruck.

"How's it?" Naina asked in a low voice.

"Fabulous! You look stunning!" Kanchan replied in a nanosecond.

Naina giggled.

"Wait, I'll do a little hairstyle." Kanchan said and walked closer to her.

"Oh my god, Naina! When did you get this bruise?" Kanchan said getting concerned after noticing a few behind her neck.

"I don't know." Naina said in a low voice.

"You can tell me."

"It's nothing, I swear. Maybe I got it that night I fell." Naina lied.

"Okay. Now go! Before you get late for your date, miss!" Kanchan said and giggled.

"Kanchan, it's not a date. He already has a girlfriend. It's all a friendly sort of a coffee which will be over like in 20 minutes and then, back to being strangers again." Naina said.

"What? He has a girlfriend?" Kanchan asked, out of shock.

"Yes."

"How do you know?"

"Eh, I overheard his conversation with her."

"Oh? You sure it was his girlfriend?" Kanchan re-questioned.

"Yes." Naina said.

Wait. Am I confident enough to state that he really was talking to his girlfriend? Naina thought to herself.

"Are you sure, you didn't misunderstand things?"

Was it really his girlfriend, or is it just me thinking? Wait. There are possibilities, that I might've misunderstood everything but, how does it matter anyway. Or does it? Naina was suddenly forced herself to stop thinking when Kanchan said something, again.

"Naina. I asked something. Where are you?" Kanchan said looking at Naina.

"Whatever, it is. I don't care. It's just a coffee. I'll be done in 20 minutes." Naina stated.

"Something tells me, things will be more to that." Kanchan said and gave her a wicked grin.

Naina ignored.

"So, Should I do your hair?" Kanchan asked.

"Is it required?" Naina asked firmly.

"Please?" Kanchan grinned and requested in a cute way.

"Okay." Naina agreed.

Kanchan combed her hair and separated it, into two sections. She combed the front section again and tucked the comb deep into her messy bun. She made a pouf of the front section and, secured it with two bobby pins.

"And, done!" Kanchan said and stretched her hands above her head as if she was tired after what she did.

"Thanks." Naina said.

"Please, that's my job." Kanchan said and giggled.

Naina did not understand so, she did not speak anything.

"So…" Kanchan said.

"So?"

"If things go wrong, in any way, I live next door. So don't worry." Kanchan said and giggled.

Naina giggled.

"Right." She completed.

"So, when you'll be done, you're invited for dinner at my place." Kanchan laughed.

"Accepted." Naina giggled.

"And tell me every detail. Okay?" Kanchan said.

"Yes, I will."

"And also, ask him if he has a girlfriend or not." Kanchan giggled hard.

"No! Obviously, not!" Naina giggled.

Kanchan laughed.

"Okay, I'll go now." Naina said.

"Off you go!" Kanchan giggled.

"Bye!" Naina said and hugged Kanchan.

"Take care and remember, if anything goes wrong and you need me, I'm just one scream away." Kanchan hugged her back and laughed.

Naina laughed, "Yes, I'll remember that one!"

Saying this, Naina walked out of Kanchan's apartment, towards her.

Naina walked inside of her apartment. She had cleaned her apartment already. She closed the door and walked inside, straight to the kitchen. She took out a pan, milk, coffee, sugar and started making coffee and some snacks to serve with it.

She then sat on the couch. She tried to relax a bit. She closed her eyes for a moment when some unpleasant and disturbing thoughts and images of her past started to appear in front of her. She squeezed open her eyes. She was unintentionally sweating already and her eyes were wet. She wiped her wet eyes and the sweat. Suddenly she noticed a name in the newspaper. She grabbed it, and it read, Reyaansh Singhania Ranked Number 2nd of India's richest industrialists. Reading this, she froze. The newspaper fell down from her hands and she couldn't breathe anymore.

All of a sudden, the doorbell rang. But, Naina was lost in her own world of tragedies. She was struck by a million of emotions. But, most of them were depressing thoughts. All of these days, she was trying to move away from her thoughts, her nightmares, her previous life, her past. But suddenly, reading one name just brought so many of the dark memories of her life which she left. Isn't it ironic? *The memories you've been trying to avoid, the ones which you locked up deep in your subconscious mind and swear in your life that you wouldn't remember any of it. But then, one song, one place, one word, one thing or one name changes things, forever. All of your hard work to move on, every little effort, seems to drift away. Seems to melt away and, you seem to be standing in the same place from where you started off.*

The doorbell rang, again. And, Naina was forced to come back from her depressing thoughts to the reality. It took her a moment or two, to realize someone was at the door. She helped herself to stand up. She walks to the door of her apartment. She again, took deep breaths and exhales, and blinks; she held the handle of the door, and pulls.

"Hi." Vivaan said and smiled.

CHAPTER-7

Vivaan was standing, with a bouquet of Forget Me Not flowers. He wore a faded blue denim jeans and a white formal shirt. His face glowed as he smiled. Also when he smiled, his eyes twinkled. He was beautiful.

"Hey. Come in." Naina greeted him.

Vivaan walked inside and took a view of the place. He didn't stop smiling.

"Sit." Naina requested.

Vivaan nodded.

He sat on the couch where Naina was sitting previously. They both sat in silence for a few minutes. Naina lost in the sudden encounter of that newspaper article and, Vivaan was trying to figure out that how he should start the conversation.

"So… um…" Vivaan cleared his throats, "How are you, now?" he completed.

"Good." Naina said.

Vivaan looked at her way. But, Naina was looking at her hands and didn't dare to look up, at his direction.

"You don't have fever now, right?" Vivaan asked.

"No."

"Okay." Vivaan said.

There was a silence, again.

"You got a really nice place, Naina."

"Thanks." Naina said in a low voice.

"Oh, these are for you." Vivaan picked up the bouquet and gave to Naina.

Naina, for the first time since he came, dared to look up into his eyes. Naina flushed scarlet but somehow managed to take the flowers from his hands. And then, their hands touched. The same, known electricity ran into her skin. She filled her chest with oxygen, in one go. Vivaan smiled because he sensed it. Naina notice, she flushed again and blinked her eyes.

For the first time, someone had the supernatural power to make her feel this alive, someone who basically made her forget the mess she was dealing with, like a few seconds ago with just one touch.

"Coffee?" She asked.

"That's what I am here for!" Vivaan said sarcastically and smiled.

Naina hopped up from the couch and walked straight to the kitchen, which was to the left of the drawing room. Vivaan followed.

"So, you're a teacher!" Vivaan asked in his childish voice.

Naina raised her eyebrows. She smiled and replied, "Yes."

"You should do that often, you know." Vivaan said.

"Do what?"

"That beautiful thing you did."

Naina lifted her eyebrows again.

"No, not this! Although, I love this as well." Vivaan said looking into Naina's deep black eyes.

Naina couldn't cope up and she flushed again.

"And, also this." Vivaan said, without blinking and staring at her like a small kid with twinkling eyes.

Naina pretended to be busy with making coffee but all she had to do was to, heat it.

"But, I love that thing you did, the most." Vivaan said.

"What…" She said very slowly, she realized that and cleared her throat, "What thing?" she completed, yet she lacked confidence as usual.

Vivaan giggled.

"Your smile, silly!" Vivaan completed.

"Oh." Naina said within nanoseconds.

Vivaan giggled again.

"I'm a lawyer, by the way." Vivaan said.

"I know." Words slipped from Naina's mouth.

"Am I that famous, eh?" Vivaan laughed.

"Wait, did you do some sort of research on me?" Vivaan said.

Naina rolled her eyes.

"Yes and the sources tell that you're a Casanova." Naina said sarcastically.

Vivaan frowned.

"Naina, I don't believe in love." Vivaan said.

For the first time after they met, Vivaan was this serious. And instantly, Naina regretted, bringing up this topic. Naina didn't answer.

"Anyway. How long have you been living here?" He asked.

"Two or three weeks, maybe." Naina answered.

"Oh." Vivaan said.

"Yes."

Naina took out two cups from the microwave in which, coffee was being heated and some snacks. Vivaan helped her with it and they both carried the coffee and the snacks to the living room, placed it on the table. This time, she did not notice the name or the article. She gave one coffee-filled cup to Vivaan and took the other one, took a sip of the coffee.

"Eeeee!" Naina screamed.

"Are you okay?"

"Coffee was hot." Naina said.

Vivaan laughed so did she.

It was the first time Vivaan saw her laughing. She looked beautiful when she smiled. As if, *all the pain that she was hiding somewhere in her heart, melted. Her eyes lightened when she smiled and made her look younger, prettier and attractive.* Vivaan couldn't keep his eyes away from her. She noticed and she flushed.

"You look beautiful when you smile." Vivaan said, getting lost in her beautiful eyes.

Naina did not say anything. Vivaan sensed the awkwardness and he cleared his throat.

"Coffee tastes great." Vivaan smiled.

"Thanks." Naina smiled.

"So, you visited the nearby places?" Vivaan asked.

"No."

"Why?"

"I… umm…" Naina choked.

"I'll take you to a place, tomorrow." Vivaan interrupted.

"Umm… I…" Naina said.

"You'll love the place." Vivaan interrupted again.

"Actually I have school, tomorrow." Naina said.

Thank God, a good excuse to avoid. Naina thought to herself.

"Okay, till what time?" Vivaan asked.

"8-4pm." Naina said.

"Great, I'll pick you up at 4:30." Vivaan said.

"Um, I do…" Naina said.

Suddenly Vivaan's phone rang. So, Naina got interrupted again.

"Hello? Hey. Yes, I know. Yeah. Okay. I know! Baby, listen to me, please? I promise I'll spend the rest of my evening with you. Okay? Please don't be mad at me." Vivaan kept repeating these sentences all over again.

What the hell?! Naina thought to herself and lifted her eyebrows.

"Listen, Sharara. I'll talk to you later." Vivaan said and disconnected the call.

Vivaan then looked at her and said, "Sorry about that, I have to go, sorry for leaving like this. Okay, so. I'll see you tomorrow at 4:30 pm. Okay?" He stands up and walks furiously towards the main door.

"Vivaan, actually that's what I wanted to tell you. I do…" Naina said before she got interrupted by Vivaan's phone call again.

"Sharara!" Vivaan answered and smiled at Naina. He waved goodbye to Naina and moved his lips to say the words sorry.

Naina nodded because there wasn't anything else she could say or do. She watched him leave, with his one hand holding his phone and walking away as he disappears from her sight.

Why does this happen every time? Why? Why does this happen that, whenever he asks to meet up, I never am able to say a 'No'? Why? That too, when he's such an ass! I mean. He's sitting in front of me, and he's talking to some other girl, and telling her that he'll spend the rest of the evening with her? Wow. In front of me! Naina thought to herself. Suddenly, the doorbell rings.

Naina walks to answer it, it was Kanchan.

"Hey." Kanchan said!

"Hi." Naina said and welcomed her inside.

"How was it?"

"Um… He asked me to meet him tomorrow as well." Naina replied.

"Oh my god! It's totally a date, Naina!" Kanchan said.

"Nope, and I'm not meeting him." Naina said and explained everything to her.

Kanchan listened to her carefully.

"Naina, I don't know. Look maybe we are wrong and he does have a girlfriend or maybe we are right and it's just an assumption because he himself has not clarified it. But in neither case, it makes him a bad person. He helped you that night out of nowhere and cared so much for you. Even if as a friend, he is there for you and I don't find anything wrong in this unless…" Kanchan stops.

"…unless?" Naina asks and raises her eyebrows.

"Well unless you like him." Kanchan said.

"No I don't like him."

"Well okay then, but if you like him and he has a girlfriend named Sharara, it'll be one hell of a problem."

"But I don't understand this that he confessed to me, that he doesn't believe in love. Then why does he have a girlfriend?"

"Maybe he doesn't."

"I don't know." Naina said.

"You know what? You should meet him tomorrow and talk to him, try to get to know him."

"I don't think it'll be a good idea, Kanchan…"

"I don't want to hear it."

"I'll think about it."

Is Kanchan right? Should I meet him once maybe? I'll try to know him and who Sharara is. Or maybe I should stay away it'll be best for both of us. Naina thought to herself.

CHAPTER-8

"Vivaan!" Savita, Vivaan's mother called out his name.

Vivaan was just heading back to his room when Savita noticed him.

"Mom, Hi!" Vivaan turned around and greeted her with a smile.

"You met Sharara?" Savita asked.

"Yes, she's far better now." Vivaan said.

"Did she eat anything?" She asked.

"She did."

"I was quite worried about Sharara. She can be very impulsive at times"

"I know."

"I got a call, they said she was angry."

"Yes. She was, because of me." Vivaan said in a low voice.

"Look, Vivaan. She's you're responsibility, you have to take care of her."

"Yes."

"Besides, I trust my son. He's a gentleman. He wouldn't do anything wrong." Savita said and hugged Vivaan.

"Did you eat anything, darling?"

"Yes."

"Don't lie. You cannot lie, to your mom at least!" She giggled.

"How do you know everything?" Vivaan giggled n return.

"I'm your mom!" Savita smiled.

"Come! Join me at the dinner table." She said.

"Okay."

They both walked towards the dining hall and grabbed the seats. The dinner was served by Scarlett. Savita thanked her and she left.

"How's Naina?" She looked at her son and smiled.

"Eh, um…" Vivaan flushed.

"I know you visited her." She laughed.

"How did you know?"

"Well that was just an assumption and I thought you would know how she is." Savita laughed.

"She's far better than that day." Vivaan said. He was kind of embarrassed.

"She's a great girl." She said and looked at her son.

"I know." Vivaan said with sparks in his eyes.

"I liked the fact, that you actually shared your room with someone; someone who was a complete stranger." She said.

"She needed it more than I did." Vivaan flushed.

"I remember, you slept on the couch while you made her sleep in your room. That's really considerate of you." She said.

Vivaan smiled.

"I like her. She's sweet." She said.

"She's sweet." Vivaan smiled.

"I know, I'd like to meet her again sometime." Savita smiled.

"Yeah, I'll ask her to come over."

"Maybe I'll ask her then what she thinks about you, too." Savita said.

Vivaan looked at her in surprise.

"Oh don't you give me those look I know what's going on in your mind and your heart lately!" Savita smiled.

"Mom!" Vivaan flushed.

"So you must be meeting her again?" Savita teased.

"Mom!" Vivaan laughed.

"Okay, okay." Savita laughed.

Vivaan smiled.

CHAPTER-9

"So, what do you think?" Vivaan looked around and then looked at Naina and smiled.

"Beautiful." Naina said.

Vivaan and Naina walked inside the entrance of The Garden of Five Senses. It was a perfect evening, with clouds covering the sun and a perfect weather. The wind was blowing, caressing Naina's hair. There was a beautiful sun clock inside the garden. It was a huge dusty brown colored clock with chocolate brown designs and was covered in grass, everywhere. The place was huge. It was like a big beautiful park. It had various theme areas, including a section on the lines of Mughal Gardens, plus pools of water lilies, bamboo courts, herb gardens and solar energy park. The garden was designed exactly to stimulate the five senses with its beauty and attractions and to give a chance to touch, smell, hear, and see the natural surroundings. There were statues of huge elephants, children praying and a bell tree. Wherever one could look, there were plants, trees etc. The place was breath-taking.

Naina and Vivaan silently explored the place, without speaking to each other, quietly enjoying the presence. *There was this silence again. There is something about silence something, indescribable- something so genuine, so warming and beautiful. Even when your lips are quiet, your heart is speaking, something only a soul can hear- someone whom you'd want to tell your secrets to, someone whose presence makes you feel calmer, composed and a better person. A person with whom you know, you don't need to rely on words, because they understand. And with that person, with that soul, you are comfortable in sharing the beauty of silence, to cherish the beauty of silence.* They both walked around, till Vivaan was tired and smiled at Naina. Naina understood the gesture and his expressions. Vivaan sat on the grass like a 5-year-old kid with joyous eyes. Naina sat beside him.

"So, Naina. You never asked anything about me?" Vivaan looked up at her.

"Tell me something about you?" Naina smiled at him.

Vivaan smiled. He couldn't stop staring at her beautiful face, her smile especially. It had left a mark on his heart.

"Well apart from being famous, I'm a good at saving beautiful ladies at 3 am from the rain." Vivaan said and laughed.

"It wasn't 3 am!" Naina laughed along.

"You look beautiful when you smile, Naina. You should do it quite often."

Naina felt conscience of herself suddenly.

Vivaan laughed noticing it.

"So, do you have any boyfriend?" Vivaan asked, changing the topic.

And, within a Nano-second, Naina froze.

"Did I ask something private? Ah, I'm sorry I didn't mean to make you feel uncomfortable." Vivaan apologized, looking into Naina's eyes.

Their eyes met, and for the first time someone was able to ease her pain, someone was able to take her out from the world of breathlessness. Naina somehow felt the same butterflies in her belly, when she looked into his eyes. *They were beautiful, beautiful than anything she has ever seen. Looking into his eyes was like, looking into the world's best painting, something which would not just please your eyes, but touch your heart and imprints your mind. And, she felt all of it. There was something, a hidden vibe, which was constantly pulling her towards him.* She was quite unsure of what kind of vibes it was.

"Uh, no, I...I don't have a boyfriend. You?" Naina cloaked.

"No, Naina. I don't have a boyfriend as well!" Vivaan laughed.

Naina laughed along.

"Who's Sharara?" Naina asked while laughing.

Wait, Damn it. What did I just asked!? Naina thought to herself and flushed.

Vivaan gave Naina a smile to comfort her; probably he understood what was going on her mind.

"Sharara..." Vivaan said. He took a gap, to say his next words for which he struggled a little.

"You know our maid, Scarlett? Her mother used to be very ill months before. And, since Scarlett's mother also worked at our house for many years, my mother and I were very concerned about her health. So, I used to go to Scarlett's house, to meet her mother very often. And then, I saw her neighbor was harassing a little girl. A man was hitting a little girl, from his belt."

Vivaan took a deep breath and said, "Naina. That girl was barely 12 years old. She was screaming in pain while he was laughing at her. I rushed inside their house, to save her. The man was drunk. And he turned towards me, asking who am I and how did I get in. But, all I could see was that little girl, who was sitting and crying in the corner. She saw me and ran towards me. She hid behind me, weeping more and more. She had so many untreated wounds, scars; I was startled to the core of my heart. That man came towards me to hit me, but I pushed him and he simply fell and remained unconscious till we walked out, with her. She is mentally damaged. No one deserves to be treated like that. That man did those things to that little girl, which Naina. I cannot even describe. She was sexually harassed at the age of 12. Her name is Sharara."

Naina could not believe her ears; the things which she was listening made her feel numb. She was constantly looking at Vivaan. She could not utter a word.

"I took her to the hospital right away. She thinks I'm her savior. Some sort of angel sent from the god, to save her from that devil." Vivaan smirked.

"How funny, right? Even when she was going through such torture, she did not lose any hope, for a better tomorrow. *Perhaps, everyone needs an angel to save them, from this scary and dangerous world.*" Vivaan said.

"You know, even today. Sharara is so afraid of people around her. She is afraid that everyone would hurt her like that man did. She told me, she never saw her parents. She was homeless. One day it was raining and she had nowhere to go. When this man came and promised her that he would take care of her and will take her to a safe place, he harassed her till the day I rescued her. She's been harassed from the age of 9 years. I just don't know what would have happened to that dear child if that day I wouldn't have saved her. Even that night, the day we met, I was going to meet Sharara then I saw you on the road helpless and groaning in pain. So I came to help you out." Vivaan finished.

They sat in silence. None of them said anything. But Naina kept looking at him.

"That look I saw in Sharara's eyes, the day I rescued Naina. That was the look I saw in my mom's eyes when I was 16." Vivaan said in a very low and timid voice.

"My mother was a victim of domestic violence for years, but she never spoke a word because of me. She did not want that I become a child without a father." Vivaan was looking down, to his hands and Naina, at him.

"I…I…"Vivaan choked.

"Hey, shh... It's alright." Naina instantly leaned and hugged him. Naina caressed his back as he sobbed in silence. Naina tried to soothe him. She herself tried to hide her tears.

"This is the sole reason why I don't really believe in love you know. I mean, ever since I was a child I have seen my father abusing my mother, them fighting. I never really saw love, happiness between them. I don't say I don't believe in *love*. I believe it *does exist*. But it *sure as hell does not exist for me.* So I never even tried. I was just too scared to give my heart to somebody like that." Vivaan said composing himself.

"Vivaan. You know, you are beautiful and I know you have been through so much, so much Vivaan. I cannot believe how you must have coped up with everything. Vivaan you helped your mother to go through the grief, you helped Sharara to go through her grief. And..."

"But no one helped me with my grief I guess. *You save everyone, you help everyone but when it comes to you, who saves you?*" Vivaan interrupted and looked down.

"Let me help you." Naina slowly caressed his cheeks. It was a sudden action perhaps a reflex.

Vivaan held her wrists and looked up at Naina with tears in his eyes.

They say boys should not cry it indicates as a sign of weakness, men should not cry it indicates as a sign of cowardliness. This is how the society thinks. I wonder whether they forgot that men are humans as well and they have 'rights' to cry if they feel to, if they want to pour their heart out they have all rights to do so. They have rights to cry to scream to take it all out to vent it all out. They are only humans. Naina thought.

"Vivaan, I know you've been through a lot and no wonder how long you've been holding onto this pain, keeping everything inside, bottling feelings inside- the pain, the anger, the rage perhaps, the tears. Vivaan, you are so strong but I understand the part that *one cannot be strong always, one have their times, the times where they need to feel pain purposely, to touch the pain and realize that yes, that pain exist, to let it consume them, only for someone to help them out, only for someone to help them to escape those feelings, and for that someone to be introduced to that pain and to allow them to heal you."*

Naina stopped as she realized she still was looking into Vivaan's eyes and his eyes were wet. She moved her fingers and wiped his tears and she smiled at Vivaan and continued, "Vivaan, don't worry now. You are not alone, ever. I'm here for you and I'll be here for you, *always*." Naina said.

Vivaan held her fingers softly and murmured, "Thank you."

Naina smiled and nodded. It was a very beautiful day, in the park. The sun was about to set. The lights were turned on. Small children came in that park with cricket bat and ball. It was perhaps a group of 10-11 small kids both girls and boys. The boy who wore red T-shirt threw the ball and the girl who wore yellow frock hit the rubber ball so hard that it somehow landed exactly on Vivaan's head and bounced off.

Naina laughed.

The girl with yellow frock made an apologetic look and all the kids gathered around each other, perhaps thinking how they should get the ball or what should they do.

Vivaan smiled at the way Naina laughed and looked at her.

"Did it hurt?" Naina asked controlling her laughter.

"It would have, only if the ball wasn't made of rubber." Vivaan said running his fingers through his silky soft hair.

Vivaan got up and picked up the ball and walked to Naina.

W*hat is he up to?* Naina wondered.

The girl who wore yellow frock finally walked to Vivaan, perhaps the kids finally decided who to send to, to fetch the ball.

"Hi, can I have the ball please?" The girl said. She smiled with her teeth trying to melt away Vivaan.

Naina laughed.

"Sure but that ball hit me real bad..." Vivaan ran his fingers through his hair again, "Ouch!" He said.

Naina was confused.

"Sorry, bhaiyya." The little girl said making an apologetic look, again.

"I'll forgive you but theirs one catch." Vivaan said and Naina frowned in confusion.

"What?" The little girl copied Naina's expression.

"I'll return the ball if you let me and didi play with you all." Vivaan said and smiled.

"What?" Naina said instantly. Vivaan shushed her.

"Okay." The little girl took the ball and clapped. She ran to her friends to spread the news.

"What was that?" Naina asked instantly.

Vivaan stretched his arm, giving her a hand to help her get up. "Come, it'll be fun." He smiled.

"I don't know how to play."

"Well I can assure you none of us know either." Vivaan laughed.

Naina looked at the children and they were happy as they would be accompanied by two more new players. She then looked at Vivaan.

"Come on, Naina." Vivaan requested with his million dollar smile.

Naina smirked, "Okay." He grabbed his hand to stand up. They walked to the kids. It was evening already and they played with the children. Naina took the bat, sometimes she missed the balls, at times she hit a 6 or a 4 but hitting the ball was very rare. Vivaan laughed and Naina laughed as well.

"The evening was amazing" Vivaan said as he dropped Naina outside her apartment.

"I had a great time as well." Naina smiled. She walked ahead and stopped, she turned around and looked at Vivaan- who was already looking at her and smiling. She smiled back at him and waved him 'a bye'. He waved her 'a bye' as well. It was dark as the moon and the stars shined bright. The light reflected on Naina's face and Vivaan couldn't stop gazing her till she left. It was a beautiful day. And, something in between them *changed*.

She decided to go to Kanchan's instead of going to her apartment. She walked to Kanchan's apartment and asked Kanchan whether she would like to come over for dinner at her apartment this time. Kanchan smiled and agreed. Kanchan and Naina cooked food together, Naina told her about her day, about how she was wrong and he indeed was an amazing person. She kept few details to herself, more like the details about Vivaan's mother and how he is upset with it and she told her the rest.

"See I told you that you should meet him." Kanchan said and smiled while eating.

Naina rolled her eyes.

"So?" Kanchan said.

"What?"

"You like him don't you?" Kanchan said.

"No I don't. And don't start it again." She said instantly and giggled.

"You're such a liar. He's a nice guy." Kanchan smiled.

Even though I want to like him, I cannot like him. Naina thought to herself.

"Vivaan." Naina said.

"Naina," Vivaan said.

"I miss you."

"Why did you miss me?"

"You have such beautiful eyes, Vivaan."

"Why did you miss me Naina?"

"I want to spend each and every second with you. I don't want you to be away from me, even for a moment."

"Why, Naina?"

"Vivaan, I don't want you to get hurt."

The place was very dark, Vivaan was lying beside Naina. They both were facing each other.

"Naina."

"Vivaan."

"Vivaan, I care about you."

"Why, Naina?"

"Vivaan. I like the way you smile."

"Why, Naina?"

"I'm scared."

"Naina."

"Vivaan, I even love the silence in between us."

Vivaan comes closer to Naina. He strokes her hair strands and looks right into her eyes.

"Naina." Vivaan said getting closer to Naina.

Naina suddenly woke up. It was night, 4 am. The room was dark but a lamp was on. That was the first time Naina dreamt of Vivaan.

And she wanted to know, the answers to the questions Vivaan asked her in sleep.

CHAPTER-10

It was morning and, Naina had to go the school. It was the first time; in her entire life, she was late. She runs and hurries to get ready. It was 7:30 am and the school would start at exact 8 am. And they wouldn't allow the teachers to come to the school later, either. She started to panic because she didn't want to take a leave since it was the last working day before holidays. She knew only one person can help her through all of it. She picked up the phone from the table.

"Vivaan." Naina said.

"Good Morning." Vivaan greeted her with a cute pleasant voice.

"I need a help." Naina said trying to concentrate how she needed to get to school on time.

"Yeah?"

Naina described the whole scenario to Vivaan in a hurry.

"Oh, don't worry I'll pick you up from your place like in 5 minutes." Vivaan said.

"Thank you." Naina said with a sigh of relief and smiled.

"Welcome." Vivaan said.

Naina was still smiling even after 5 minutes passed after she talked to Vivaan. Probably, it was just a little silly excuse to meet him again. Probably it's just that she heard his voice in the morning. *There's something extra-ordinary about these things. When we hear the voice or see the people we love in the morning, it just makes the rest of the day so happening. It induces such high amount of positive vibes that the rest of the day passes by as amazing as we want it to be.*

After a few minutes, Naina was completely ready. Naina wore a simple plain red saree, with her hair open, jhumkas and a silver wrist watch. Suddenly the doorbell rang and an instant smile came on her face. She looked herself into the mirror *and first time after all these years, she smiled back at her reflection.*

"Hey," Naina looked at Vivaan and smiled.

Vivaan looked at her and was mesmerized. "Hey," Vivaan managed to speak up and smiled.

Naina locked her apartment and walked with Vivaan to his car.

"Ready?" Vivaan smiled and look at her.

"Yeah," Naina smiled and answered.

Vivaan and Naina reached the school but unfortunately, at 8:10 am. The watchman refused to open the gate. And Naina frowned.

"Sorry madam, rule is same for both student and teachers. I can't help it."

"Damn." Naina said.

"It's okay."

Naina sighed deeply.

"Naina."

"Vivaan."

Vivaan smiled trying to make her smile. Naina gave a faint smile.

"Since you missed your school today, perhaps you can come with me? Like, spend some time with me?" Vivaan asked.

Instant happiness spread across Naina's face yet she tried to show herself as calm as possible.

"Would you like to meet Sharara?" Vivaan asked while he was running his fingers through his hair.

Naina was mesmerized the way he looked so charming and so beautiful without even trying, she smiled and said, "I'd love to."

They both walked to Vivaan's car.

"So, Naina what kind of songs are you into?" Vivaan asked as he changed the radio stations while driving.

"Any." Naina smiled.

"Any?" Vivaan giggled.

"Yes." Naina giggled as well.

"Don't you like talking? Or is it because of me?" Vivaan giggled.

"What?" Naina laughed as she tucked a few hair strands behind her ears.

"You're beautiful." Vivaan said and smiled.

Naina flushed.

"Okay, so I have to buy something so I'll be back in a minute or two." Vivaan said as he parked the car near a grocery store.

"Shall I come along?" Naina looked at Vivaan, and their eyes met. She couldn't look at him for too long as there was something in him that always made her conscious and made her heart skips its beats.

"Sure." Vivaan said grinning.

What a perfect set of teeth. Naina thought to herself and smiled at her silly thoughts.

They went inside, the store was huge, bright and there were lots of racks where the products were kept. There were a lot of people buying groceries. Vivaan walked straight and Naina followed him.

"Chocolates!" Naina said and smiled looking at Vivaan.

Vivaan laughed at the way Naina acted so childish.

"Sorry." Naina giggled.

"I assume you like chocolates, as well?" Vivaan asked.

"Like? I love chocolates." Naina laughed.

Vivaan smiled and noticed each and every little detail of Naina's expression. Naina was transforming slowly, but for good.

"Who else like chocolates?" Naina asked with twinkling eyes.

"Sharara." Vivaan smiled at this new, carefree look of Naina.

Naina smiled back.

Vivaan bought lots of chocolates for Sharara and kept them in a small paper bag.

They walked out of the store to their car.

"Why don't you take one?" Vivaan said looking at Naina pointing out at the bag of chocolates with his eyes while driving.

"Okay." Naina said and smiled.

Naina un-wrapped the chocolate bar and ate a piece. She didn't realize that the piece of the chocolate was so big that it completely filled her mouth. She felt awkward and tried to gulp it all down when the liquid chocolate escaped from her lips and cascaded all the way down to her chin. Feeling conscience she wiped it all from her tongue, leaving more stains of the chocolate in entire of her mouth. She felt more awkward. She tried to take a glimpse of Vivaan wondering if he was witnessing her stupid and silly acts, and to her surprise, Vivaan was already looking at her with an awe expression with a smile on his face.

Naina flushed.

Vivaan smiled at her to soother her consciousness and said," Naina, Sharara isn't alright. She fears everyone who she doesn't know, would take her away to that hell, again. She is kind and sweet to the people she recognizes but, can be dangerous the people she doesn't know. I don't want you to get hurt."

A slight sadness hit Naina's face as she tried to keep her expression constant, somehow Vivaan noticed it.

"Naina."

"Vivaan."

"Naina."

"Vivaan."

Vivaan grinned at her and said, "Would you let me take a piece of your chocolate as well, cherry blossom?"

"Cherry Blossom?" Naina asked and giggled.

"Your new nickname," Vivaan giggled.

Naina laughed.

"So does that mean that I'll get my share?" Vivaan laughed.

"Yes." Naina grinned and blinked her eyes.

CHAPTER-11

Care for You Rehabilitation Centre was a huge building located in a vast area around beautiful surroundings which were full of nature, trees, animals around. The weather was pleasant, and it was calm and quite unlike the city.

"The place is beautiful." Naina said and smiled at Vivaan.

Vivaan sighed in awe.

"Yes." Vivaan smiled back, noticing the details of her expressions.

Naina looked around the place.

"Naina, listen." Vivaan said.

"Yeah?"

"I want you to give these chocolates to her." Vivaan said and gave the bag to Naina.

Naina smiled and nodded.

Vivaan smiled back.

They both walked into the building, the building had a garden at the entrance and there was a help desk in front of the entrance. Everyone waved Vivaan and smiled at him, Vivaan smiled back. It looked like he knew everyone.

Vivaan obviously knew the room where Sharara lived, so Vivaan walked through the corridors passing 5-6 rooms, Naina simply followed him. And then, Vivaan stopped in front of the room number 26. Something happened to Vivaan and he couldn't enter the room.

"What happened?" Naina asked in a low and soft voice.

"I'm afraid, Naina."

"Of?"

"That, when I'll go inside the doctor would tell me that there is no progress in Sharara's health."

"What makes you think that?"

"I don't know."

"Vivaan, *if you don't open the door today, you'll always be curious about what could be inside it.*"

Naina placed her palm of her hand on Vivaan's shoulders and said," It'll be okay. Trust me." And she smiled.

Vivaan took a deep breath and opened the door.

And, there she was little Sharara, on the bed with her caretaker. The caretaker was reading her a story and she was listening to her very carefully. Suddenly Sharara looks at Vivaan and all her expressions changes. She smiles and runs towards Vivaan. Vivaan spreads his arms and hugs Sharara tightly.

"I missed you." Sharara said and didn't leave Vivaan for the next five minutes.

"I missed you more."

"Liar,"

"No, I did miss you!"

"Why didn't you come and meet me then?"

"I'm sorry."

"What will I get if I forgive you?"

"Well, I have something for you."

Sharara looks at Vivaan with twinkling eyes.

"Naina," Vivaan said as Naina walked in front of Sharara who was standing behind Vivaan all the time looking at them with awe.

Sharara frowns but stays calm. She does not utter a word.

Naina gives Sharara the chocolate bag and Sharara takes it.

The caretaker and Vivaan were shocked to see Sharara behaving so nicely with a complete stranger.

Sharara opens the bag to find lots of chocolates. As soon as she sees them, a huge smile spreads on her face. She suddenly hugs Naina. Naina hugs her back with a smile.

"You're beautiful, I like you. Thank you." Sharara said giggling.

"I like you too, welcome."

"I'm Sharara, Vivaan's sister."

"I'm Naina. Vivaan's friend."

"Friend?"

"Yes." Naina smiled.

"Or girlfriend?" Sharara giggled.

Naina smile awkwardly but became speechless.

"You're one hell of a mischievous lady aren't you?" Vivaan laughed at Sharara.

"Lady with a class, mind you!" Sharara laughed.

Everyone laughed.

The lady doctor walked into the room.

"I see everyone's getting along well, here?" Doctor smiled.

"Very! I got chocolates! See?" Sharara showed off her chocolates to the doctor and grinned.

The doctor smiled, "Yes, but don't finish them in a day, and also share with everyone. Okay?"

"Okay." Sharara exaggerated the word and chanted the word in rhyme and laughed.

"Can I talk to you for a minute, Vivaan?" Doctor said.

"Sure!" Vivaan said happily and looked at Naina in a way to ask her to come along with him and Naina nodded.

"I'll be back, okay princess?" Vivaan said and kissed Sharara's forehead.

"Okay." Sharara smiled at him.

"Naina, you'll come back too right?" Sharara asked.

"I will." Naina said and smiled.

"Yay!" Sharara exclaimed happily.

Vivaan and Naina followed the doctor as she walked to her cabin.

"Take a seat please." The doctor said.

"Any problem, doctor?" Vivaan asked.

"No, this is a positive thing for us at the moment." Doctor said.

Vivaan smiled hard and he couldn't control his emotions and he didn't realize when he placed the palm of his hand on Naina's wrist.

"I did not expect her to talk so nicely to Naina and everything to go so smoothly. It's a good sign." The doctor continued. "Vivaan, I want you to take her to some new place. Some place near nature."

"Since she has recovered 78% from our reports, the conversation with Naina will totally make it to 82%. At this stage of treatment, we prefer to take the patient out somewhere or the family members. Generally, we insist the family members do so, but today mostly family members leave the patients to get rid of them. But here, Sharara's case is different and you're taking care of her the most. And since, she has a scope to recover completely; you must take her out somewhere. When she'll go out, interact, see other people and children of her age, there are possibilities that her brain would suppress the fear and trauma she went through completely."

"Doctor, I'll take her. I don't have any problem." Vivaan said.

"Naina, can you go with them as well?" the doctor asked.

Naina gave a surprised look.

"Naina, believe me. From the day she has been with us, there is no person she has talked to properly. It's either me or the caretaker or Vivaan. If someone tries to talk to her, she screams and tries to hurt them with any possible thing- from scissors to the glass vase. But today, communicating to you has probably helped her brain to release a hormone oxytocin which helps someone to trust. If you'll be along with her, she'll easily be able to move on from her past."

"I... I..." Naina choked.

"We'll see it later, it's up to Naina. We cannot force her. I'm glad that you're taking Sharara out. Her improvement is all because of your love, care, and attention Vivaan." Doctor said.

"It's all because of your hard-work, doctor." Vivaan smiled.

"No. Well, yes I cannot say that the medicines and therapy were not one of the reasons. But, a patient seeks not just for a medical care, but also love and support of the family. If the patient realizes that they do not have his family or a guardian to support them, it mentally damages them and the healing becomes slower comparing to when the patient knows he is loved and gets all kind of attention and support. I've seen such patients but this case was different. I'm proud of you." The doctor said and smiled.

Vivaan smiled.

"Do tell me a day earlier, and the dates you decide to leave." The doctor said.

"Yes." Vivaan said.

CHAPTER-12

After talking to the doctor, Naina and Vivaan spent the whole afternoon with Sharara. When it was time to leave, Sharara hugged Vivaan and Naina.

"You'll back, right?" Sharara asked Naina.

"Yes." Naina smiled.

"I like you very much! I'd like to see you again." Sharara said with twinkling eyes.

"I'll come to you, soon." Naina smiled and kissed her cheeks.

"Bye!" Sharara smiled and waved.

"Bye!" Vivaan and Naina said.

They both walked out of the building back to the car. They both didn't say anything, on the way back to Naina's house. Naina thought about Sharara, her sweet smile, the things she had to go through. And then, she thought about how she wanted to help Sharara from that phase where she is stuck. *A phase where she needs someone to pull her out from the melancholy she was surrounded with.* Vivaan pulled over, bringing out Naina from her thoughts. It was evening and the moon already took his place. The moonlight fell on Naina's face, brightening up her eyes.

Vivaan couldn't stop staring at her. Naina flushed. Vivaan smiled at her expression.

"It was a beautiful day today. Thank you for spending your time with me, Naina."

"Vivaan."

"Naina."

"I want to help Sharara."

"Naina, I…"

"Shh…" Naina dismissed his words and continues, "Vivaan."

"Naina."

"I want to help her. Let me help her."

"How?"

"I want to come along."

"Where?"

"Anywhere."

"What do you mean?"

"Anywhere you go."

Naina and Vivaan were staring right back at each other's eyes as the moonlight fell on their faces.

"Naina, you know you don't have to do this."

"I want to do this."

"Why?"

"…because I could feel a connection between Sharara and me." Naina said maintaining the eye contact and said, "I really want to help her, Vivaan. I mean if you allow me to. Please." Naina completed.

It was some kind of strong connection Naina and Vivaan made that Vivaan melted. Naina's eyes face, the way she spoke- Vivaan couldn't stop looking at her.
Naina flushed. Vivaan smiled again.

"Okay." Vivaan smiled.

And, there was an instant smile on Naina's face.

"But where should we take her? I mean which hill station?" Vivaan asked.

"I know."

"Which?"

"Manali."

"Manali?"

"Yes."

"You've been there?"

"Yes, a place which makes me feel so peaceful." Naina smiled.

"So, get your bags packed. We'll leave tomorrow."

"Tomorrow?"

"Yes."

"What time?"

"I'll call." Vivaan smiled.

"I'll wait." Naina smiled back.

And for a minute, Naina forgot everything. She was living a beautiful life. She was happy and finally she was *breathing*. She walked out of the car to her apartment.

It'll be a hell of a day, tomorrow. She thought to herself and smiled.

CHAPTER-13

It was a beautiful evening. Naina was completely ready with her bags packed. She was sitting on the couch in the hall as her phone vibrated with Vivaan's number. It was the fifth or sixth time they were talking on the phone since yesterday. Naina didn't complain.

"Hello?" Naina said with a smile on her face.

"Hi, it's me." Vivaan said from the other side.

"Hey."

"You ready?"

"Yeah"

"Okay, I picked up Sharara already and I'm on my way to your apartment. We'll go to the bus stand directly."

"Alright,"

"You got your bags packed?"

"Yes."

"Okay, I'll come up, to pick the luggage for you."

"Thanks."

"See you."

"Bye."

Saying this, the call was disconnected.

Naina lay back and closed her eyes. She was quite tired since she could not get a chance to rest since the plan was made all of a sudden. She took a deep breath and let it out and relaxed her body with the same. Kanchan helped her to get her all the stuff; she gave her few dresses to keep as well. After a minute or two, the doorbell rang. She walked towards the door and opened it. It was Vivaan.

He wore simple sweatpants and a hoodie and a pair of spectacles. He looked charming. Naina couldn't stop looking at his beautiful and well-defined features.

"Hi!" Vivaan smiled and waved at her breaking Naina from her thoughts.

"Hey." Naina said.

"How are you doing?"

"Excited, and you?"

"Good, me too," Vivaan smiled.

"How about Sharara?"

"She's good as well. She just doesn't stop talking!"

Naina giggled. Vivaan joined.

"So, where's the luggage?" Vivaan asked.

Naina located him where the bags were kept, they both walked out of the apartment after Naina locked the flat properly. She knocked Kanchan's apartment to inform her she was leaving. She hugged her and bid her goodbyes with a promise to return soon, and to bring gifts.

Through the elevator, they came out of the building to the car. As soon as Naina opened the gate of the car, Sharara hugged her from her waist.

"I'm so glad you're accompanying us to Manali!" Sharara smiled.

"I'm glad, as well!" Naina said looking down at Sharara as she caressed her cheeks.

"Come sit with me!"

"Yes." Naina said.

Naina smiled and nodded at the caretaker who also accompanied them on the trip. Everyone sat in the backseat, while the driver drove them to the Bus stop from where they had to board the bus to Manali. It was late in the evening when they reached. The conductor of the bus helped Vivaan to keep their luggage inside the bus. It was important for Sharara to sit with the caretaker and the bus offered only two seats simultaneously, so they all decided that Sharara must sit with the caretaker and Vivaan and Naina will sit together, so they did. After half an hour, the bus started its journey for Manali. Naina occupied the window seat while Vivaan sat by the aisle.

The bus was spacious, semi sleeper with an LCD TV with a DVD player. The windows were sealed shut, as well. Later, the conductor played a movie on the T V. While others enjoyed the movie, some people decided to sleep, or talk. Sharara engaged herself with talking to her caretaker and Vivaan while Naina fell asleep.

Vivaan couldn't stop looking at how someone can look so beautiful effortlessly. Naina was wearing sweatpants and a normal graphic shirt with her hair open and a small pendant around her neck yet, she looked stunning. *The light fell on her face making it glow. Her skin shined into the light. Her hair looked like silk and her lips moist.*

Even with the movie playing, and with so many people talking, Vivaan could feel only Naina, as if there were only two of them on the bus. Due to a few jerks, a few strands of Naina's hair fell on her lips. Vivaan slowly moved his fingers towards her face and moved the hair-strands away.

Suddenly the bus conductor stopped the movie and said loudly that they were going to take a break of 1 hour. Whoever wants to get off for a while can totally use up the opportunity.

Vivaan got conscious and took his fingers away suddenly as soon as Naina was waking up from her little nap.

"I want to eat noodles." Sharara looked at Vivaan.

Vivaan giggled.

"Okay." Vivaan said.

Everyone got off the bus, some people walked around, some had dinner, some were clicking pictures and some were stretching. Road trips can be a real annoying thing just the way it can be enjoyed so much. But you see when you have to sit for long hours in a same position it does not sound very appealing idea. Everyone got out of the bus. They had stopped over a restaurant which was beautiful. There was a staircase that led you further, at left there were two small shops that served milkshakes and snacks, at right there was a gift shop. And in the middle was the entrance to the restaurant. There was a small water fountain, swings and multiple iron chair and tables for people to sit and relax. There was also a speaker attached and randomly songs were playing.

Sharara listened to the song as started swinging her hands in the air and runs towards Naina and smiles. She knew the song and it looked like it was her favorite. Sharara eye-signaled Vivaan and looking at Naina and started lip syncing with the song.

Kehta hai pal pal tumse hoke dil yeh diwana,
Kehta hai pal pal tumse hoke dil yeh diwana

Sharara then turns at Vivaan and sings her next part,

Ik pal bhi jaan-e-jaana mujhse dur nahi jaana,
Pyaar kiya toh nibhaana,
Pyaar kiya toh nibhaana

Vivaan and Naina both laughed from the way she danced. She was carefree. She did not care much of how people were there, that might were looking at her. She did not feel cautious, she enjoyed on what life brought her. Maybe that's how kids are. Happy and carefree- unlike adults who stress over little things and keep themselves always burdened.

The songs kept playing Vivaan and the caretaker brought food as Naina sat along with Sharara and talked how cold it was. Sharara sat in the middle of Naina and Vivaan. They all talked when it was the time for Sharara to take her medicines.

"Oh, don't worry I'll bring some water." Naina said as she got up and signaled Vivaan to sit and relax.

Vivaan smiled and nodded.
Naina walked to the counter and asked for a glass of water. She turned and looked at Vivaan. He was cleaning Sharara's mouth with napkin as he smiled and listened to Sharara describing her characters of her favorite Disney movie. An instant smile came across Naina's lips. She noticed the change in the song and listened to the lyrics of the song as she looked at Vivaan laughing.

Tum yun miley ho jabse mujhe
Aur sunehri mai lagti hu,
Sirf labon se nahi ab toh,
Poorey badan se hasti hu

She could somehow relate to the lyrics. She felt those words. You see when we are feeling an emotion, any emotion; we are able to relate to the words, music, art, books, anything which describes it perfectly. We drown in those songs, words, or say world of fiction completely, because it understands us even though it's vice versa of it. Ever since she met Vivaan, her life wasn't completely changed, but some part of it was. Naina wasn't completely changed but she slowly was turning into a different person- a happier person, a better person.

The waiter brought a glass of water which distracted her from her thoughts. She picked it up and walked to Vivaan and Sharara. Sharara took her medicines and walked around while Vivaan and Naina sat together. The wind caressed Naina's hair as she looked and smiled at Sharara. Vivaan couldn't stop looking at her. *Sometimes, it's just so amazing how people you just meet become such crucial part of your life. How all you think is never letting them go away. How all you think is keep them in front of your eyes and read everything that's going in their mind and their heart, to notice every little detail of their faces- how they smile, how they laugh, the way they look when they frown or when they are upset. You just don't want to let go off their presence as it makes your heart feel warm. It makes you feel whole and complete.*

The bus conductor honked as a signal for the passengers to return to the bus. Everyone walked back to the bus. Sharara and the caretaker went inside the bus. Naina looked at Vivaan as she remembered the further lyrics of her new favorite song.

Mere din raat salone se,
Sab hai tere hi honey se,
Yeh saath hamesha hoga nahi,
Tum aur kahi mai aur kahi...

~

After a while later, the bus started its journey towards the mountains. People who were using phone were disappointed as they reached a "No Network" zone.

Naina, who was back to her sleep, Vivaan himself was too tired, so he fell asleep as well. The caretaker gave Sharara a more few medicines and they both fell asleep as well.
Naina woke up with the honks and noises. She opens her eyes to see, Vivaan. He was asleep, facing her. His face looked calm and composed of a small little innocent child sleeping beside her. She couldn't help but look how irresistible Vivaan looked at that very moment. A little smile came over her face.
He looked like what moon looks to fireflies. They want to touch it, feel it, but cannot.

Let me see your beautiful colors from a distance and smile. Let me just sit here and watch you fly. She thought to herself. *Perhaps, some feelings are never meant to be realized.* She closed her eyes, for these new feelings which she tried to avoid. She took and deep breathes and exhaled. She turned her face around and opened her eyes. Suddenly she slapped her palm of her hands on Vivaan's hand.

Not only she slapped his hand, but also grabbed it and held it tightly. The tight grip woke Vivaan up, he looked at Naina. Naina was looking at the window.

"Naina?" Vivaan said. He was worried.

Naina did not respond. She only held his hand tighter than before.

"Naina?" Vivaan asked again.

Naina did not respond again.

Vivaan was worried now. He took his hand and placed it on Naina's shoulder.

"Naina?" He said softly.

Naina moved her head towards him slowly. She had her eyes shut tightly. And her lips pressed inwardly. Vivaan looked at her and he was blown away by her beauty. She looked scared but looked amusing. A small smile rushed into Vivaan's face.

"What's wrong?" Vivaan said, looking at her as he smiled.

"Heights... It's... I'm scared of Heights." Naina chanted the words as she held his hands tightly.

Vivaan smiled.

"Naina… Shh. I'm here." Vivaan said.

He placed his other hand on her hand.

"Open your eyes, Naina." Vivaan said.

"I... I... Can't," Naina said.

"Trust me."

Naina opened her eyes slowly and found Vivaan's eyes already staring at them.

"I'm here." Vivaan said.

They both looked into each other's eyes, without saying anything. It was the very first time Naina could hold her gaze on him. They didn't say anything. A sudden jerk broke the eye contact and Naina squeezed shut her eyes again.

Vivaan giggled.

"Naina," Vivaan said.

He moved his fingers towards her cheeks, but he stopped midway. Naina tightened her grip on Vivaan's hand. Vivaan finally caressed Naina's cheeks with his fingers. Her cheeks were soft and chubby. Naina slowly opened her eyes again.

"Shh." Vivaan said.

Naina looked into Vivaan's hands. She was scared so much that she had no idea what was going on.

"Look at them!" Vivaan pointed out towards the window while he caressed her cheeks.

Naina refused by moving her head left to right.
Vivaan slowly pushed Naina's face upwards and their eyes met for the third time. Vivaan moved his fingers near her lips, "Trust me." He said.

Something was in his eyes that made Naina believe him. She blinked her eyes in approval and Vivaan smiled. She slowly moved her head towards the window in the direction where he pointed out.
And all she could see were a billion or more stars shining back at her in the deep black sky.
Naina was mesmerized by the beauty of each star which was shining so bright and the moon looking brighter than it does usually.

A smile came instantly on her face. She looked at Vivaan, with wide open eyes and a huge smile on her face,

"Do you see them? They are so beautiful oh my god!" Naina said.

She turned her head back to the window and said, "I'm so blessed that I'm alive to witness such beauty!"

Vivaan looked at her and said, "I feel blessed to witness such beauty as well." And he smiled.

Naina loosened the grip, yet she was holding his hand.

"Do you know my grand-mother used to tell me that the one, who dies, becomes a star and takes care of us, like a guiding angel." Naina looked at Vivaan and smiled.

Vivaan smiled but was speechless. He couldn't get over the innocence of her soul. There was such beauty in her thoughts and purity in her. He couldn't get over how beautiful she was inside out. Naina turned back her sight to the beautiful stars. And, Vivaan turned back his sight to Naina. None of them realized when they fell asleep, Naina's head on Vivaan's shoulder and their hands intertwined.

With this, the fear which grew so deep in her heart was, freed.

CHAPTER-14

It was early in the morning when they reached Manali. Vivaan and Naina were still sleeping in the same position.

"Good Morning!" Sharara screamed.

It suddenly woke up Naina and Vivaan and also other passengers who started staring at Sharara. Sharara didn't bother to notice the awkward stares.

Naina realized that her hands were still clasped into Vivaan's. She suddenly took her hands away from his. There was a little awkwardness. Her brain gave her a little flashback to last night and she blushed crimson.
Vivaan yawned and stretched his arms a little and everyone got off the bus one by one.
Vivaan claimed their luggage and he walked back to Naina, Sharara and her caretaker.

Since they got down the first thing that hit them all was the cold chilly breeze. Naina shivered. The place was beautiful. The air was fresh, pollution free. It was cloudy and the wind was a little harsh. There were mountains, pine trees, birds were flying away from their nest in search of food. Local people were covered with wool and caps. The bus driver had dropped them on the Manali bus depot where all the buses were parked. There was a taxi stand along with it and the mall road was adjacent to it.

"Here take this." Vivaan came closer to Naina and placed his hoodie on her shoulders.

Suddenly the wind blew Naina's hair and a few of her strands fell on Vivaan's face. Sharara grabbed Naina's hands to show her something and forced her to walk with her. And, Vivaan had his eyes closed all of this time.

Why do your eyes close when you kiss or cry? Because sometimes, all your heart wants is to feel, those feelings. That's all. Perhaps, that was a reflex action made by Vivaan's mind, making his eyes close and feeling how it is to feel Naina's hair on his face, the smell, and softness of it.

"Vivaan! Aren't you coming?" Naina said, holding Sharara's hands.

Vivaan slowly opened his eyes.

"Yes." He said.

Naina smiled at him and started walking further with Sharara and her caretaker. They took a taxi and went straight to their cottages.

"I thought we are staying in a hotel." Sharara said.

"I thought that too, but you don't get a feeling of being at home in hotels, right?" Vivaan smiled at Sharara.
"A cottage," Naina smiled looking at them.

There was a small entrance with an iron gate. She walked inside to discover more of its beauty. Sharara followed her. She walked straight and saw there were two cottages on the left, and four on the right. Two cottages were built side by side. There was a swing, in front of the left cottage.

Sharara screamed, "This is where I want to live!" In a childish rhythmic tone and kept repeating it.

Naina laughed at her. She turned towards Vivaan who still was standing in front of the small hut shaped reception with their luggage, staring right back at Naina and smiling. Naina smiled back at him.

Minutes later of talking to the person in the reception, a person carried their luggage and led the way while Vivaan followed. He walked straight to the left cottage where Sharara was playing in the garden with her caretaker.

"Right now, only one cottage is available. It'll be available after 12 pm." The person said.

Vivaan nodded.

"Is there any other thing which I can help you with?" The person asked.

"No, thank you." Vivaan said.

Naina was standing beside Vivaan. Sharara and her caretaker came inside the cottage as well.

"I'm sleepy, I'm hungry and I'm bored. But, I'm hungry, more." Sharara said grinning.

Naina and Vivaan laughed. I'll order something, till then you all change and relax.

"Okay." Sharara said.

Vivaan looked at Naina, Naina nodded. They both exchanged smiles.

Vivaan walked out of the cottage to order food, while the caretaker helped Sharara to take a bath and gave her medicines. Naina went into the bathroom for the shower.

The bathroom was big; it had a huge mirror and a sink. Naina opened her clothes. She notices her scars. The bruises were healed, but the scars were still, there. Her brain forced her into the flashbacks of the past, the unwanted memories of the past. Suddenly she felt breathless. She inhaled harder and harder. She walked towards the shower and opened the tap. She fell to the floor. The hot water touched her scars. She covered her face with her palm of her hands and she cried without making a sound. *That's thing, even though you want to move on from pain, you want to move ahead of the things that breaks your heart, it doesn't leaves you easily. It stays with you, like a dark entity slowly consuming you, eating you. No matter how happy you are in one point of your life, the darkness, the hollowness within your feel, is something which is latched itself within your soul. The happy thoughts, the happiness, it's what the exterior things provide you- say the new movie of your favorite actor or a baby's laughter. But when you are alone and you are with yourself, you feel that pain. You feel it because it's not an exterior feeling, it comes from you, and it lives within you.*

"Naina, are you okay?" The caretaker said after knocking the door of the bathroom.

Naina was inside the bathroom for the past 2 hours and didn't come out. Getting no response, the caretaker knocked again,

"Naina, are you alright?" She said with a slightly higher pitch.

"Ye... Yes." Naina replied a few seconds later.

"Um, okay I'm taking Sharara out in the garden. Okay?"

"Hmm," Naina replied.

Naina was still on the floor with her legs pressed close to her chest and her hands locking them and her head resting on her knees. She grabbed the tap and closed it. She wiped her face and walked towards the towel and wrapped her hair. With another towel, she dried herself and wore clothes. She wiped her face with the palm of her hands again and took a deep breath and exhaled. *Even though wounds heal, a scar never leaves you. They stay behind telling you a story or reminding you a story. Reminding you either you are brave enough to defeat it or weak enough to be defeated.*

She opened the door and walked out of the bathroom when she slipped. She closed her eyes thinking she'll fall. She did fall but in Vivaan's arms. The towel, with which she wrapped her hair, fell. She opened one eye and saw Vivaan holding her hands and her waist, and looking straight into her eyes. She blushed and she looked down. Vivaan helped her to stand up.

"You okay?" Vivaan asked.

"Yeah, thanks." Naina said.

"Naina, Naina, Naina!" Sharara ran into the room singing and chanting Naina's name.

"Naina, let's go and play!" Sharara requested.

"No, Sharara. You need to sleep. It was a long journey. You can play after the nap." Caretaker said.

"I hate naps." Sharara said.

Poor Sharara had no idea how much people value the sleep after they grow up.

"I'll sleep on the couch for the meantime." Vivaan said looking at Naina.

Naina smiled in acceptance. Everyone went to sleep since they were tired from the long journey. The chills in the air, the room heater, and a soft blanket made a perfect combination to pull everyone into a good sleep.

~

Later in the evening,
Naina was the first one to wake up. It was dark already. She opened her eyes and rubbed them like a small baby waking up from her nap. She yawned and walked out of the bed. She wrapped herself in her woolen shawl. She walked out of the room and saw Vivaan sleeping on the couch. She walked closer to him. The drawing room was cold. She sat on the chair, in front of him. She observed him while he was sleeping.

He looks so beautiful she thought to herself. Something got into her and she stretched her arms towards his cheeks, and caressed it. His cheeks were cold, but still, *it was still his skin*. They were so soft. She walked back to her room, took the room heater, and placed it near Vivaan. She covered his hands with the blanket which slipped down.

She walked out of the cottage and sat on the chair. The view was beautiful. It was dark, yet visible. The mountains were dark blue in color, and the mountains hiding behind them were almost black. The snow on them reflected a sky blue color.

A little cute puppy was sitting near the table in front of her cottage. He was probably shivering. She took the shawl and wrapped the puppy with it. And then, she sat on the chair again.

"You know you have such a beautiful heart, Naina." Vivaan said who was leaning by the door, observing her actions with a smile on his face.

"Thanks." Naina said, smiling. She tucked a few strands of her hair behind her ears.

"Enjoying such a great view, huh?"

"Yeah, Manali's beautiful."

"Yeah," Vivaan smiled.

Vivaan sat beside Naina.

"So what's your story?" Vivaan asked.

"My story?"

"Yeah,"

Naina gave him a complete blind look.

"Your story, Naina. Like about you, the real you. Not the one you show you are. The one who loves chocolates and loves stars." Vivaan looked directly into her eyes. Naina stared back at them for a minute and blinked.

115

There was something in him, which attracted her so strongly. But she was afraid of something so she resisted.

"It's getting colder; I think we should go inside."

"Naina,"

"Vivaan,"

"*I can see you and I feel you, these depressed and sad eyes? I bet once you must've been so happy. I know you'll find that feeling again.* And trust me when I say this Naina, It'll be beautiful. *You just need to listen to your heart, and breathe. You must live your life without any fear. Laugh like no one can hear you, cry like no one can see you, share things like it's the first time you're sharing or it's the first time happening with you, listen to your heart like it knows it all, and love like you never knew heart breaks.*"

Vivaan had said something which kept Naina awake all night. Naina was getting closer to Vivaan. From day one, she felt this strong connection. There was something in Vivaan that was changing Naina.

But still, the broken parts of her were hard to heal. She was broken to that point, that even if she tries to think about trusting anyone with her heart, the past memories would torture her to death. You see, a person always knows how he can heal himself. But how do you silence the mind?

She wanted to surrender to these feelings she felt in her heart but the pain resisted.

CHAPTER-15

"Where should we go?" Vivaan asked as Naina sat in front of her with the caretaker and Sharara sat beside him.

"It's a beautiful place we can go anywhere. I bet Manali has so much to offer." The caretaker said.

"Yeah, she's right. There are many places we can visit." Naina said.

"So where is our guide didi taking us?" Sharara said as she stuffed pancakes inside her mouth and looked at Naina.

"Let's go to Van Vihar, it's a park here." Naina said.

"Yeah, I can go to a park!" Sharara said and grinned.

"Guess that's the place we're going first, then!" Vivaan smiled.

After they finished eating pancakes and coffee, at a restaurant Naina knew in the "Mall Road Market". They walked out of the restaurant. The markets were long and full of crowd. Sellers were selling their products while costumers bargained with the prices. Some were eating ice creams while some were having momos, in both ways people enjoyed summer and winter both. They walked to the Van Vihar.

It wasn't very far from the restaurant they were in. It was barely few steps away. Vivaan bought the tickets.

117

Everyone walked in. Van Vihar was beautiful. There were plenty of Pine Trees all over. Sunlight made its way to touch the ground, even when the trees were getting on its way. There were plenty of swings so Sharara ran and captured one swing before any other kid could. Naina walked ahead and looked around, Vivaan followed. The caretaker was asked to take care of Sharara who somehow managed to find more kids and started having a conversation with them.

"It's beautiful, right?" Vivaan said.

"Yeah," Naina smiled.

"Thanks for coming Naina; I cannot even imagine managing all of it without you."

"You don't have to be thankful, Vivaan. You know I wanted to come. I wanted to help Sharara in any way I could possibly help her. Besides, there are holidays in my school and I would have been bored if I stayed back."

"So I should be the one thanking you for letting me come with you all." Naina grinned.

"Sharara really likes you." Vivaan said as he looked at Sharara. She was now sitting on a swing and talking to a girl with pink frock and pony tail.

"She's sweet." Naina looked at Sharara while she pointed at them and waved. Probably telling another girl with whom she came here.

"So tell me your hobbies." Vivaan looked back at Naina and giggled.

Naina giggled at the way he sounded. "Well, I like travelling."

"I'm sure about that one since you're the one who brought us Manali." Vivaan smiled.

"What else?" He added.

"And, I love writing." Naina said.

"Really? You write?"

"Well, I try to. Not very good at it, trust me." Naina said.

"I cannot trust you my lady until I read or hear your work." Vivaan laughed.

"No... Like, really I don't..." Naina said as Vivaan interrupted her.

"I insist. Please." Vivaan said with his million dollar smile.

Oh, only if I knew how to say a no to that smile of yours. Naina thought to herself.

"Okay. I've written this one long back ago."

"Yeah, go on..."

" *Na jaaney unki palkon mein neend kaisey aati hogi, Jab dil unka jaanta hai, Ki kisi ki ankhein unki bewafai se, Roz raat nam rehti hai.* " Naina completed.

Vivaan kept looking at Naina. Vivaan looked into her eyes, looking for answers he may never find. He tried to

119

look deep into her eyes wishing he would find the cause of the aches, wishing he would find all the places she has been hurt- so that he would heal them. But sadly, he found nothing but emptiness.

"...I, I can't find the right words." Vivaan managed to say.

"I told you I'm not that good." Naina smiled.

"No, it's not that I don't like it and I'm not able to find words. It's that I love it and I'm wondering if it would be right to fit it into a single word. It's beyond words."

"And if you could fit your emotions into words which you felt after listening to my small poem, what would it be?" Naina asked looking at Vivaan.
"Heart breaking, and beautiful," Vivaan said and smiled.

Naina smiled back.

"Would you like to wear the traditional bridal dress of Manali?" A lady asked and smiled at Naina. There were many people who were making out a living through these things. Few people gave bridal wears on rent to click photographs, some asked whether they'd like to hold a rabbit and click a photo, and the others gave colored wigs on rent.

"No, no. Thank you." Naina said.

"Why not? Try it on." Vivaan said.

"No, really,"

"Come on, Naina. You'll look great."

"But..."

"Wait, I'll ask Sharara to join you, as well."

"But, Vivaan..."

Vivaan calls out Sharara and she heard him at once. She ran and reaches Vivaan within a fraction of seconds and her caretaker had to run and chase Sharara.

"Do you want to wear a bridal dress?" Vivaan said grinning at Sharara.

"Yes!" Sharara grinned back and looked at Naina, as well.

"So what do you say now?" Vivaan looked at Naina and laughed.

"Please be my partner, as I have no groom right now?" Sharara said and made a cute face which was hard to say a no to.

Naina sighed, "Okay." she said.

The lady wrapped Naina and Sharara into a red cloth and, tied a belt and safeguarded it with pins. A silver necklace and a scarf with big silver earrings were a part of their clothing as well. All of this time when Naina and Sharara were getting ready, Vivaan was standing with his back in front of them. He was checking updates on his phone.

"Vivaan?" Naina called out his name.

Vivaan turned around and he was mesmerized. Naina looked beautiful in the bridal look. Her open hair added the charm in the look. Vivaan couldn't take off his eyes from Naina. He couldn't resist from smiling. She looked perfect.

"Let's click pictures!" Sharara said.

Sharara's voice brought Vivaan back to the real world from his reel one. Vivaan clicked plenty of pictures, of Naina and Sharara. He asked the caretaker to click the picture of them; he then walked beside Naina and asked Sharara to stand in the middle.

"Wait, I'll click a picture of you both, as well." The caretaker said looking at Naina and Vivaan.

Sharara walked away, and Vivaan and Naina smiled for the camera.

"Get a little close. You're not fitting completely in the frame." Caretaker said.

Vivaan walked closer to Naina and stretched his hands to hold her. He leaned in towards her.

"May I?" Vivaan whispered?

Naina nodded and smiled.

He held her by her waist and but took a few seconds to gaze at her. He could smell her scent. *It was the most amazing feeling.* He thought.

Caretaker in the meanwhile clicked pictures of them.

"Beautiful." The caretaker said looking at them and then at the photos.

Naina flushed.

They walked further towards the "Beas River". They clicked more pictures.
The sound of running water gave, Naina some kind of a peace. It was like she had any kind of a relationship with this place. It soothed her to that extent that it relaxed her mind and made it stress-free. Naina, Vivaan, Sharara and her caretaker were sitting on the stones near the river. Naina's hair strands were blowing in the direction of the wind she kept her eyes closed as the wind touched her skin. The beauty and the peace of her mind brought a smile on Naina's face. *There's this thing about nature it knows ways to compose your mind and restless soul.*

Vivaan clicked Naina's pictures secretly, without telling her. She looked so beautiful, that he wanted to capture every color of her into his camera. *He wanted to photograph her and keep her safe with him forever.*

After spending some time, on the shore of the river, they finally returned.

"There's a temple, we should visit." Naina said.

"I don't actually, believe... I guess, I told you. I'm an atheist." Vivaan said.

"It's okay. I'll go." Naina said.

"I'll come along!" Sharara said.

Naina smiled at her.

"You should come, too." Naina said looking at Vivaan.

"Naina, but..."

"Vivaan. You know everything in this world depends upon hope. And, in this life, we cannot be alone, always. We need someone. We want someone. To tell them how our day was, to share our problems. For some people, that someone is the God. And coming to temples, churches or monastery gives them strength to fight the odds of their life. And, a person who has no one, they have the God." Naina said and smiled.

Vivaan was speechless. He simply looked at Naina. He was standing and had no words to say.

"So, what do you say now?" Naina grinned.

"I'll come." Vivaan smiled.

The temple was big. It was completely made up of wood. It was beautifully made. The temple was situated in the middle of the "Van Vihar". The long trees and mountains, the sunlight added beauty to the temple. Removing their shoes, Naina went inside and Vivaan, Sharara followed Naina. Naina closed her eyes and prayed while Vivaan watched her details. Sharara copied Naina. After praying, they came outside.

"What did you wish for?" Vivaan asked, looking into Naina's eyes.

Naina looked at Vivaan, and she smiled.

"I cannot tell you."

"Why?" Vivaan asked curiously.

"Secret," Naina laughed.

Vivaan smiled looking Naina smiling.

"What did you wish for?" Naina asked.

"Secret," Vivaan laughed.

"I wished for chocolates, you know." Sharara said and laughed.

Naina and Vivaan laughed along.

"I'm tired." Sharara said.

"Let's go back then." Vivaan said and smiled at Sharara.

Everyone returned back to the cottage. It was a long and tiring day. They ordered food.
Vivaan and Naina watched Disney movies which Sharara asked them to watch along. And later, after having the dinner, Vivaan walked back to his cottage and everyone went back to sleep.

If I could only ask one thing today, please make me live this day twice. I want to see her as a bride again. I want to see her as my bride, again. Vivaan smiled as he thought of his wish he asked in the temple he slowly drowned in sleep.

CHAPTER-16

In the morning, they planned to visit, 'Rohtang Pass'. The place was quite far from Manali. The journey was of 3-4 hours straight. So they decided that they'll travel by cab.

Everyone went to get ready for the journey. Sharara was quite excited. It didn't take her more than 15 minutes from changing her clothes to cheering everyone to get ready as fast as they can. After getting ready and eating their breakfast, everyone walked to the car and left for Rohtang Pass.

Sharara borrowed Vivaan's phone to play games and to listen to songs, while Naina was still sleepy. Naina was sitting in the middle, Vivaan sat on the front. Looking at Naina Sharara felt sleepy too. Sharara sat quietly as she was very sleepy. She rested her head on Naina's shoulders as she caressed it with her eyes closed. Vivaan looked at them in awe.

The taxi driver stopped the taxi for a while when Sharara woke up she looked up at Naina and asked where Vivaan was. Vivaan walked inside the car with a white plastic bag. He turned around to see everyone was awake now. Vivaan smiled and passed the white plastic bag to Sharara.

"Chips! Thank you Vivaan, they're my favorite red flavor!" Sharara said.

"There's green too, for Naina." Vivaan giggled.

"How do you know green ones are my favorite?" Naina raised her eyebrows in surprise.

"Secret," Vivaan said and giggled more.

Naina smiled and opened the packet.

"There are chocolates as well!" Sharara said with a huge smile.

"You have to share them with Naina; she loves chocolates just as much as you do." Vivaan looked back at Sharara and smiled.

"You didn't have to mention that, she's my didi I will always share things with her." Sharara frowned.

"And, I'll always love you for that." Naina said and smiled as she hugged Sharara closest to her chest and kissed her forehead.

"We're almost there; we'll take half an hour break here." The cab driver said, stopping the car.

They all walked out of the cab. There was a small restaurant, they walked inside.

"I want to eat Noodles." Sharara screamed out of joy.

"Again?" Vivaan laughed.

"*Food is the only source of eternal happiness. Everything else is fake.*" Sharara said.

Vivaan gave her a blank look and burst out of laughter

"You're such a little drama queen." Vivaan said.

Naina smiled listening to their conversation.

"It's so cold, here." Vivaan said, looking at Naina.

Naina was sitting on the chair and Vivaan took a seat for himself, as well.

"It is." Naina said, folding and rubbing her arms.

"Hey have my jacket." Vivaan said.

"No... It's o..." Before Naina could say anything, Vivaan took off the jacket and covered her with his jacket.

"Thank you." Naina said.

Vivaan smiled.

"What would you like to have?" A man with a notepad came to their table.

"Would you like to eat something?" Vivaan asked looking at Naina and the caretaker.

They both shook their heads in denial.

"Okay. Two cups of coffee and one plate of noodles please." Vivaan ordered.

"Okay." The man left.

Vivaan's phone started ringing.

"Hello?" Vivaan answered it.

"Hello." The other person answered.

"Mom! How are you?"

"I'm good. How are you? How's the trip?"

"I'm good, as well Mom. And yes, the trip's going very well."

Sharara calls out at Naina, and they both walk out of the restaurant towards the car and Sharara takes out a notebook from her Disney princess bag and shows it to Naina.

"How's Sharara?"

"Sharara's recovering."

Naina and Sharara started laughing about something which Sharara said. Vivaan was continuously looking at Naina with a huge smile on his face.

"How's Naina?"

"She's beautiful, Mom." Vivaan said.

After two seconds of realizing what he has said he panics,

"Oh! I mean, she's absolutely fine. She's playing with Sharara at this moment."

Vivaan's mom laughs.

"You like her don't you?"

Vivaan looks at Naina from the window and Naina looks back at him.

"*I think I'm falling in love with her.*"

"That's amazing, Vivaan. Naina's a great girl. I like her too."

The waiter arrived with the food and then he placed it on the table. Looking at it Sharara rushes inside and Naina follows her.

"Mom I'll talk to you later, okay?"

"Take care."

"I will." Saying this Vivaan disconnected the phone.

Vivaan joined them all on the table. Naina smiled at Vivaan in a way to assure everything's okay or not, Vivaan understands and nodded and smiles back. After finishing the food, they resumed their journey to Rohtang Pass.

There was a lot of traffic on the road. The road was narrow. The path was a little dangerous but was worth it. The mountains looked beautiful, and they were spread widely. And after a while, they reached their destination.

Rohtang Pass was beautiful. There was snow, everywhere. Sharara was so happy to the snow that she stepped out of the car to touch the snow. But as soon as she did that, she was hit with the cold wind.

"Damn, it's so cold." Sharara said, folding her arms.

Naina smiled.

They all walked out of the car and looked around. There were many more tourists who were clicking pictures, skiing, walking around, and playing with the snow. It was very cold.

"I'll pick you up from here; if you need anything you have my number." The driver said as Vivaan nodded in agreement.

Sharara started playing as she made snowballs and started hitting at Naina and Vivaan.

"Sharara, no. No, don't do it." Naina said.

She stepped back as Sharara threw the balls on them. And suddenly Naina tripped and fell on Vivaan who was just behind him.

"Haw, sorry." Naina said getting up.

Vivaan laughed, "Don't worry its okay."

"It was fun, isn't it?" Sharara laughed at them.

After spending an hour, Vivaan and Naina helped Sharara in making a snowman.

"I'm not feeling well, Vivaan." Sharara said.

"What happened?" Naina looked at her and Vivaan walked close to Sharara.

Naina checked Sharara's body temperature and she had a high fever. They all rushed back to the cab. Vivaan sat along with Naina as he was worried for Sharara. The caretaker gave some medicines to Sharara, while Sharara tried to relax herself, and within few minutes, she slept like a baby. Everyone was tired. Naina closed her eyes and fell asleep after a few minutes. Unconsciously, she relaxed her head on Vivaan's shoulders.

A smile came to Vivaan's face. It was a beautiful feeling for him, to experience. *He could feel her breaths, while she was sleeping.* He felt it. The feeling was divine.

As they reached the cottage, Vivaan took Sharara into his arms and made her sleep on the bed.

"You should sleep, and take care of Sharara." Vivaan said and smiled as heading back to his cottage.

Naina nodded in agreement. It was a long and tiring day, but not as tiring for Naina to smile at Vivaan every time he smiled.

CHAPTER-17

It was early in the morning when Vivaan woke up. He got dressed and walked to Naina's cottage. The caretaker opened the door.

"How's Sharara?" Vivaan asked.

"She's not good enough to be taken out." The caretaker said.

"Oh." Vivaan said frowning.

"You can go with Naina." Sharara said.

"I didn't know you were listening to our conversation, Missy." Vivaan laughed.

Sharara laughed as well.

"Don't ruin a day because of me, please. Take Naina along with you." Sharara said.

"But, Sharara..."

"No, I'll feel bad then. That I ruined the trip."

"Okay. I'll take her."

"Where are you going?" Sharara asked out of curiosity.

"Salong Valley,"

"Sounds romantic," Sharara laughed.

Vivaan pouted.

"Tell her that you love her today."

"What? No! I don't love..."

"Of course you do. I'm not dumb." Sharara laughed more.

"Tell her before it's too late," Sharara grinned.

Vivaan rolled his eyes.

"At least tell her today's plan."

"Oh, yes. Where's she?" Vivaan asked.

"In the room,"

"Okay."

Vivaan walked into the room to find Naina still sleeping. She was covered in the blanket and looked so calm and composed while sleeping. She looked beautiful. Vivaan sat beside her. And he kept looking at her. He remembered how she sounded while she slept. Her rhythmic breaths while she slept sounded like music, a kind of music while gave peace to Vivaan's soul. The sunlight escaped from the curtains and fell on Naina's face and broke her sleep. She opened her eyes to find Vivaan sitting beside her. Naina had her eyes wide open now and was speechless and slightly awkward. Vivaan stood up within a fraction of a second.

"Oh, I came to tell you that we're going to Salong Valley today." Vivaan said.

"I didn't know Sharara recovered this soon." Naina said rubbing her eyes.

"No, actually it'll be just you and I."

"Huh? What about Sharara?"

"She doesn't want us to waste our day because of her."

"It doesn't matter."

"It does to her. If we won't go, she'll feel bad."

"She can't stay alone."

"She won't be alone. She has a caretaker. And I arranged pizza and her favorite Disney movies for her."

Naina laughs.

"When do we leave?"

"In an hour?"

"Okay."

"So does that mean you're coming?"

"Yes." Naina smiled.

Vivaan smiled back.

Naina was ready to leave after an hour. She wore a red dress, with ankle length boots and open hair. She always loved keeping her hair open.

Vivaan was spell bounded the way she looked- so gorgeous. The dress was a knee length dress that revealed her perfect soft legs and her flaunted her figure. Her hair was silky soft which blew was the wind touched them. She had a black colored jacket in her hand and a bag.

Naina caught him staring.

"What?" She smiled and asked.

"You look so beautiful, Naina."

Naina blushed. They both walked to the car, after saying goodbye to Sharara After 30-40 minutes of driving, Naina and Vivaan reached Salong Valley. The route was same for Rohtang Pass and Salong Valley but there was a diversion on the road and the straight road took them to Salong Valley. They walked towards the entrance. There was a passage that led them to a huge park look-alike place. Everywhere they looked, green trees and blue skies stretched their legs wide. There were small cafes and ticket booking place. There were food stalls and stable for horses. And photographers were clicking pictures of the people landing after their paragliding.

Naina and Vivaan walked to the ticket counter. Vivaan bought the ticket and they went up to wait for their trolley lift. As their ride came, they walked inside and the lift closed. They relaxed as the trolley went up in the mountains slowly and steadily. Only two trolleys could run on one go. They clicked pictures of the beauty of nature. And from such height, everything looked so pure and serene.

The trolley reached its destination and they finally walked out of the trolley. There was a cafe in front of them they walked ahead and there were lots and lots of trees, flowers- a perfect place for a picnic. The wind blew slightly with a little presence of heat of the sun. It made a perfect combination both.

"Come let's sit in the café." Vivaan said.

"Okay." Naina smiled.

They both walked to the café as Vivaan and Naina sat down, the waiter came and asked what they would like to have. Vivaan looked at Naina in way to ask what she'd like to eat.

"Coffee, momos and noodles?" Naina smiled.

"Perfect." Vivaan grinned and asked the waiter to bring all the things she said.

"So do you like it?"

"Like what?"

"This place obviously." Vivaan giggled.

"Like? I love it!" Naina smiled.

"I tell you it feels more like a coffee date." Vivaan laughed.

Naina laughed and said, "Guess your date doesn't look that bad."

"Oh you don't know how gorgeous my date looks." Vivaan said looking into her eyes and smiled.

Naina flushed.

The waiter brought them food and served on the table. Vivaan smiled at the way Naina enjoyed the hot coffee, and ate noodles and momos like a small kid.

"Don't worry I know the concept of sharing." Naina laughed and signaled Vivaan to eat.

Vivaan smiled.

"Naina," Vivaan said.

"Vivaan,"

"I need to tell you something."

"Go ahead." Naina said.

"Not here. Come with me."

As they had already finished their food, Vivaan got up and walked out from the café. He turned around and waited for Naina and he smiled. Vivaan leads the way while Naina followed. Vivaan walked down the mountain crossed the huge big pine trees, to the dead end of the park. The ends were surrounded by trees and lots of trees. There was no one and the place was completely isolated.

Vivaan turned around facing Naina looking straight into her eyes. He walked closer to her. He could feel her breath quickening. Vivaan smirked. He stretched his arms and caressed her cheeks.

"Naina, I've been feeling things from the day I first saw you. The way we met in the rain. How I couldn't see your face but then the light of the thunder made your face glow like something so beautiful yet, dark. This bond, this shivers through the spine, the quickening of breathing, the butterflies, the goosebumps, the connection between us, Naina. *You know, this world, is big and huge. But, we met. And it might be cliché but I believe we met for a reason. And the reason is what you and I feel within our heart. The feeling we behold in our skin when we see even a glimpse of each other.*

I've seen your eyes. They're so sad. As if they've seen something they never meant to see. Something you never should've felt. But, let me try. I need to try I want to try, Naina. I must, to fix you. *Because, whenever I see you, there's this irresistible urge to love you so hard that you would want to live your whole life twice.* But just, with me, because I'm in love with you, Naina. *And, I want to love you. And I can only do it if you let me do it. I want to give your heart, its heartbeats again to make you feel alive once more.* Naina, I strongly do not believe in love quoted as relationships which these young generations have come upon with. The 2-3 month of love, and if they face any problem, instead of dealing and facing it together they choose the easiest way out, to walk away from the love saying they are not compatible with each other.

Naina, *to me, love is quiet. Love is generous; it sure is serene and pure. It's never jealous or selfish, it can never be. Love means fighting, every day but not against each other, for each other. Loving means comforting each other; when you're all down and are left with no energy to maintain the rhythm of the world.* Naina, *loving means no matter how far you go, you know you need to come back to home, and home is none other than your better half, the love of your life. It's not restricted to just a term 'relationships' it's just so beyond that.*

And, I want to feel this kind of love with you. I want to make you mine forever. *Will you marry me*, Naina?"

Naina instantly took a step back. She covered her mouth with her palm of her hands in shock. Her eyes were wide open.

"Naina?" Vivaan said.

Naina turned her back on Vivaan. Vivaan walked towards her and kept his hands on her shoulder. She shoved it away.

"Naina what's wrong? I know you love me."

"What made you think so?" Naina asked.

Vivaan was speechless.

"Vivaan I don't love you. You've always been my good friend."

"Good friend? I've always been a good Friend?" Vivaan walks to her in a rush and holds her tightly with both of his hands on her shoulder.

"You think I'm an idiot? I've seen the way you look at me Naina, the way your body reacts to my touch. You can lie but not your eyes. I know you love me." Vivaan says screaming.

"I don't love you!" Naina says shoving his hands away again and walking away from him.

"Prove it," Vivaan said.

Naina was now speechless.

"Prove that you don't love me. Because I know you do! Else prove me wrong."

"Vivaan,"

"Naina,"

"I don't have to give any explanations or reasons for it."

"Really?"

"Yeah,"

"Your one false statement affects my life as well, Naina."

"I don't love you. I'm sorry." Naina said.

She turns around and starts walking back when suddenly Vivaan grabs her hand and pulls her towards him. Vivaan holds her tightly.

"Let me go!" Naina screamed.

A few tears rolled down her cheeks.

"You're crying?"

"Let me go."

"Look at me, Naina," Vivaan said.

Naina kept struggling to escape from his strong hands.

"Look me into my eyes and tell me you don't love me and I'll let you go." Vivaan said.

Naina looks him into his eyes. She opened her mouth but she couldn't say a word. As if her brain accepted her command but not completely. She looked away. More tears fell down her cheeks.

"I got my answer." Vivaan said.

Vivaan released his arms to set her free.

Naina didn't say a word.

"What's the problem, Naina? If you love me, then why can't you accept it?"

Naina didn't say a word.

"Is there someone else in your life?"

Naina didn't say anything.

"Talk to me Naina. Please."

"Vivaan,"

"Naina,"

"I'm married." Naina said as she wiped the tears.

CHAPTER-18

Vivaan was shocked. As if suddenly someone flushed out whole oxygen from that very place. He was not prepared for anything like this. He couldn't even think that something like this would happen even in his wildest dreams. He didn't know how to react. He stood there, pale and numb.

Naina turned around and saw him. But something was so different about him, now as if his whole personality changed within a second. He didn't say anything, and she didn't dare to say anything. They both went back to the cab. All the way back to the cottage, they did not speak to each other. As if Vivaan was still in shock and Naina trying to resist the fact that she broke his heart.

As soon as they reached the cottage, they both parted their ways. Vivaan went back to his cottage and Naina went to hers.

Naina went inside to find Sharara on the bed eating a large pizza and drinking a cold drink. She was watching some movie on the laptop.

"Naina!" Sharara screamed in happiness. She jumped out of the bed just to hug her.

"I missed you." Sharara said.

"I missed you too." Naina said.

"How was it, then?"

"Everything was great."

"Where's Vivaan?"

"In his cottage,"

"Did he confess?"

Naina looked at Sharara blankly. *Did she know as well? What should I say to her?* Naina thought to herself.

"Or... Maybe not! Okay, I want to meet Vivaan. I'll be back in a minute." Sharara said.

"Actually he was very tired, so why don't you meet him after an hour or so?" Naina said thinking he probably would need privacy after what happened back up in the valley and he wouldn't be able to explain everything to Sharara.

"Okay." Sharara said and hopped back onto the bed.

Naina was blank completely. She lay back on the bed and closed her eyes. She didn't realize when she fell asleep.

"Life is giving you another chance, Nidhi."

"Maa?"

The place was dark. Nothing was visible.

"Nidhi, Don't do what I did. Else you'll be lost forever."

"Maa, where are you! Please come back to me. I need you."

"Nidhi, don't lose him."

"Maa, I miss you. I need you."

The voice starts to fade out as Nidhi runs to chase the voice.

"Nidhi…"

Nidhi keeps running to chase the voice.

"Listen to what I say. Listen…"

"Maa! Maa, where are you, maa." Nidhi screams.

The voice starts to sink in.

"Don't do what I did. Else you'll be lost forever."

Nidhi stops.

"Don't do what I did. Else you'll be lost forever!"

Nidhi falls down to the ground.

"You can't leave me like you did back then! YOU CAN'T LEAVE ME AGAIN!" Nidhi shouts her lungs out.

"Come back…" She sobs.

She closes her eyes as tears fell down her cheeks. Everything was falling apart and even though she tried her best to keep up with things, she couldn't. She did her level best to catch up, to stop the person with the voice so that she could make them stay but couldn't.

"I love you, Maa." Nidhi whispered.

"I love you so much." Nidhi said.

"I need you back maa. I want you to be with me." She said with small voices.

"Lost… Forever…" The voice whispered faded completely.

"Maa!" Nidhi screamed her lungs out.

Naina woke up suddenly with her horrifying dream.

"Are you okay?" The caretaker asks.

Naina doesn't reply.

The caretaker brings a glass of water.

"Here." The caretaker says as she hands the glass of water to Naina.

Naina drinks the water with shaking hands.

"Naina, is everything alright?"

"Y…Yes." Naina said in weak and shivering voice.

"What about Vivaan?"

"What about him?"

"I don't know he hasn't shown up after you both came back and when I went to ask about whether he was okay and would like to have dinner, he did not respond to my questions. When I was leaving, he just said one thing that we're leaving tomorrow. And when I asked at what time we will leave and if he'll like to have his dinner, he didn't say anything."

"Oh."

"I'm concerned, you know. I've never seen him like this. You both really became close to each other these days. Can you like talk to him once?"

"I…I don't think…"

"No, really! You should talk to him once."

"Okay." Saying this Naina walked out of the bed and walked out of the cottage to see Vivaan sitting outside his cottage on the chair.

He was looking up at the sky, gazing at the stars. His cheeks were still wet with the tears.

We teach all the boys to be brave so that, they grow up into a brave man. We teach them not to cry. We teach them that, "Boys don't cry." That if you cry, the society would consider you weak like a girl. But, why is there such discrimination between the boys and the girls? Does crying tell you how strong a person can or cannot be? If a person cries, it's an emotion. It's a human tendency to let out the negativity from the body which is completely normal. And, crying doesn't make anyone weak. It prepares the brain to be stronger than before.

Naina walks to Vivaan and sits beside him.

"You did not eat anything?" Naina said slowly.

Vivaan didn't say anything.

"Please don't cry."

Vivaan looked at Naina, straight into her eyes. Vivaan's eyes were wet.

"Leave." Vivaan said.

"Why do you love me so much?" Naina said.

"It's okay, Naina. Maybe we'll meet again. One day, Naina when things are not this broken and I'm not so

jealous that you're not with me. Maybe one day we'll be right for each other and it won't be so hard for you to fall in love with me. I really wish that one day we'll be able to connect again because no one has ever made me feel in quite the way your presence makes me feel. But I know that day isn't today. Today you're not ready and I'm too pushy. Today we don't seem to work out and as much as I care for you, I can't keep pretending that we do. So I'm saying goodbye. But maybe one day, I won't have to. And that day, things wouldn't have to end this way." Vivaan looked away as tears rolled down his cheeks. He stood up to go back to his cottage when Naina grabbed his hands.

"Leave my hand, Naina."

"Vivaan,"

"I said, leave my hand!" Vivaan shouted.

Naina didn't leave his hand.

Vivaan looked at Naina, and Naina was looking down on the floor. She was sobbing.

"You said what you wanted to back up there, Vivaan. You confessed what you felt." Naina said.

She looked up at Vivaan and holding the eye connection, "You wanted to know my story, right? I'll tell you today." she said.

CHAPTER-19

(PAST)

"Nidhi! Get up. Else you'll get late for your job interview!" Suchitra, Nidhi's grandmother said.

Suchitra walks into Nidhi's bedroom to find she was missing.

"Nidhi! Where are you?" She said worrying.

Nidhi walks out from the bathroom completely ready. She wore a white shirt which was tucked into the black pencil skirt she wore with her hair tied up into a ponytail and a silver metallic watch.

"Have you seen my spectacles?" Nidhi asked while collecting the folders and her bag.

"No."

"Oh, there it is!" Nidhi collects the spectacles from her dressing table.

"How do I look?" Nidhi asks and smiles.

"Pretty." Suchitra said in awe.

Nidhi wears her black heels and kisses on Suchitra's cheeks.

"Let me see Maa once before I leave." Nidhi said.

Suchitra nodded in acceptance.

Nidhi walks to Shruti's room. Shruti was on the bed laying. It was Armaan's (Shruti's husband) room.

"Maa," Nidhi walks in, towards Shruti.

It has been years, Shruti lost her business. She was betrayed by one of her own employee who was offered more money by the rivalry company. And they tricked her investing in a wrong company due to which she had a big loss. She not only lost their company but also bungalow which had Armaan and Shruti's memories, which belonged to Armaan. She met with an accident. And she went into coma. Since she lost everything, she lost the will to recover from the coma as well. Somehow Suchitra and Nidhi invested their savings and everything they had to get the house back which once belonged to Armaan and Shruti thinking, Shruti might get better if she stays in that house. But sadly, *if it has to happen no matter what we do, we can never get it otherwise.*

"See, your Arti. Arti is here, Maa. I grew up so big that today I'm going for my very first job interview."

Shruti was lying on the bed lifelessly.

"You know, I've always treated you like my mother after what happened in the accident, where my mother and father died. It's you who took care of me and helped me to grow into such beautiful person inside out. It's you. You're the reason for my strength, Shruti. You're my mother, my aunt, my sister. I love you, Maa. I just want one thing, today."

Shruti was still, like always.

"I've never asked anything from you, Maa. Today, I want one thing- your blessings, Maa, just your blessings to my success today, Maa. Please wake up and wish me luck." Nidhi requested as tears rolled down her cheeks.

"You know everyone says that you wouldn't be able to recover," Nidhi choked. She wiped her tears and holds Shruti's hands.

"But don't worry I'll never give up on you. I'll never give up on the thought of you completely recovered."

"I believe that you will be fine one day, Maa." She completed.

Nidhi stroked away few hair strands that came on Shruti's eyes.

"I'll always love you, Maa. I can never completely repay for everything that you've done for me. You gave love to an orphan. You made her taste what a mother's love can be. What it is is like to be in a home." Nidhi sobbed.

"Please be okay, Maa. We need you."

"Nidhi…" Suchitra said sweetly.

"Yes, Oh I'm coming yes." Nidhi said wiping her tears away.

She looked at Shruti one last time and said, "Don't worry Maa, I'll work and get money for your treatments. You will be fine and well one day. We will all be together like before."

Nidhi walked out of the room towards the main gate.

"Bye, I'll come early as possible!" Nidhi says to her grandmother.

Suchitra smiled and said, "You know her blessings are always with you. She loves you. Do your best."

Nidhi smiled and nodded.

After traveling for 2 hours, and 15 minutes Nidhi finally reached her destination. The building was in the combination of white and silver in color. The Singhania Industries was mentioned in block grey letters.

Nidhi sighed. Wow. This is beautiful. She thought to herself.

"Please wait in the waiting room please." The receptionist said with a smile.

"Yes." Nidhi said with a smile.

The place was huge, walls were painted white. The receptionist desk was also white colored. There were white leather couches and a silver and glass chandelier above.

Looks like the people here really loves white. Nidhi thought to herself and giggled.

There were 3-4 people more who were waiting for their turn. A few were nervous; others were going through their resume and questions again and again.

Wow. People are so nervous. That's crazy. They won't eat you. Basically, they don't even know you. Even if you utter something wrong, they cannot haunt you till death. Nidhi thought.

"Nidhi Arti Bhaweja?" The receptionist calls out Nidhi's name.

"Yes."

"You may go now." The receptionist said.

Nidhi grabs her folder and her resume and gets up towards the cabin where the interview was taking place.

She enters the cabin with her eyes down, holding the folders and then she looks up to see a pair of eyes already looking at her in awe.

"Hello. Please take a seat." He said.

"Yes." Nidhi said sweetly.

He had hazel colored eyes and well-defined jaws. He was well built and dark blonde hair. He wore a black shirt and his sleeves were up till his elbows. First few buttons were open of his shirt.

This man literally doesn't really know how to appear in the interviews. Never mind, I need this job. Naina thought to herself.

The cabin was again completely white in color and the desk was completely arranged. There was no sign of any other color. All of the colors were dull. Either it was grey or white and silver.

"So, Nidhi, what thing in this world makes you believe in humanity again?" He asked.

"Um," Nidhi was all confused as the question was completely unexpected from the point of the interview.

He smiled, "Just trying to know you."

"Love," Nidhi said.

"Love?" He asked looking deeply into her eyes as Nidhi broke the connection and looked away.

"Yes."

"Okay. There is a notebook and a pen. Write me something which should include a heart-break and love both."

"What?" Nidhi said in shock.

"Go ahead." He gave a stern look.

"Okay." Nidhi said in acceptance.

She took the notepad and took a pen. She relaxed. *Nidhi you need this job for treatment of Maa. This guy is weird but you need this job. Show him the writing skills; he'll get impressed, maybe.* Nidhi thought to herself.

She kept the notepad on the table and held the table with both of her hands and pulled herself, the moving chair moved in the direction of the table. She rested her elbow on the table while she took the pen into her mouth. She kept on thinking what she can write to impress this man to give Nidhi the job she's craving for.

She then suddenly realized something and a smile ran all over her face. She wrote something on the notepad and looked up at the interviewer to realize; he was already looking at her and smiling.

Nidhi flushed. She gave the notepad to him.

"His glimpse made my day, his smile made me shine. We had love in between but it was only mine."

He looked up as soon as he finished reading but doesn't say anything.

"You like it?" Nidhi asks squeezing her eyes.

"What do you think?"

"I believe you loved it."

"I love your confidence."

Nidhi smiled.

"You're hired."

"What? Really? Like because of the quotation I wrote? " Nidhi said.

"I wanted someone with good understanding on every level."

"Oh, alright,"

"What was the toughest decision you ever had to make?"

"My mother is in coma and the doctors said there's no use of continuing further treatment. Either I could give her up or I could try hard."

"What did you decide then?"

"I decided to try even harder. Nidhi gave a faint smile.

"And on scale of 1-10, rate me as an interviewer."

"8."

"Wow that brutally honest."

Nidhi nodded and said, "So when can I join?"

"Tomorrow 9 am."

"Whom would I be working under?"

"Me, of course,"

Holy shit. Why this creep? Why not someone else? Nidhi thought to herself.

"I'm sorry I don't know your name." Nidhi said and smiled.

"Reyaansh," He smiled.

CHAPTER-20

"What? You're going to work with Reyaansh Singhania?" Suchitra asked.

"Yes!" Nidhi said.

Nidhi and Suchitra were on the dining table eating food. Nidhi had finally returned home and she was exhausted by the travelling and the interview.

"I can't believe it! I'm so happy for you!"

"I can't say I'm completely happy because…" Nidhi stopped in between.

"Because," Suchitra gave her a confused look.

If I tell her I got hired over a love-heartbreak quote I wrote for him while the new boss kept staring at me, she wouldn't let me do this job. I can't tell her this. She thought to herself and sighs.

"What?" Suchitra said.

"Nothing, tomorrow is my first day," Nidhi tried to fake her best smile.

"You must be nervous." Suchitra said.

"Not very much but yes I am a little bit."

"Don't you worry darling you'll be just fine."

"Thanks nani."

"You know Armaan was such a confident little boy when he was young."

"Tell me more." Nidhi looked at Suchitra and smiled.

"Well, he loved his drama classes. He was so good with acting, the way he used to play his roles and his parts-they were brilliant. So was your mother, Nidhi. She was so confident and full of new ideas. Our business only got better and better ever since she joined."

Nidhi smiled. She listened to Suchitra with keen interest. She wondered if she'll be as good as Shruti ever.

"At what time do you leave?"

"8 am because I have to reach till 9 am."

"I am so happy and proud of you, Nidhi!"

"Finally we can resume Maa's treatment."

"Nidhi, you know better."

"No."

"There's no scope that Shruti will ever be fine again."

"But we can still try!"

"There's no point. She's in coma from years and is on ventilator for breathing. She's practically dead, Nidhi!"

"How can you give up so easily?"

"I'm sorry. I didn't want to give any false hope."

"I have to wake up early. I'll go to sleep."

"Take care." Suchitra said.

"Yes, I will." Nidhi said and left.

Nidhi walked straight to her bedroom and she closed the door. Her room was small, not very spacious. The iron bed was huge which crème white bedcovers and bed warmer. There was a striking blue dream catcher near to her bed; to she had kept it to keep all the bad dreams away. To the left she had a wooden table and a chair with a green board covered with drawings, sketches, photographs above it. And at right she had her dressing table and a mirror which was covered in yellow fairy light and a cupboard along with it.

She sat on the bed and laid back. She closed her eyes and thought to herself. *Sometimes the hope to be reunited with the people we love is the only hope that keeps us going on in our life. We love them so much that it breaks our bones to even think they are not around us anymore. It leaves us breathless or in a void where we are alone with the most destructive feelings. This hope, that the people we love or the person we love will come back into our lives again, it makes us fight all the everyday battles. It makes us think, everything is worth it. Sometimes you just can't let go. You cannot let go of that one person you thought, will always be there for you. You just can't move on. You cannot give up on them as the love you feel in your heart is so strong that even if you're tired and you want to run for the hills- it makes you wait. It makes you feel that no- everything will be alright one day and you will again cherish the taste of being together, even when it's not true. The heart at times tries to find the easiest and the shortest path for you to walk. But you can never hold onto the things that are temporary. You can never hold onto air while falling, you know if you don't grab something stronger, you'll fall and get hurt. Perhaps, life works in the same way.*

Naina felt heartbroken as whatever Suchitra said was nothing but the harsh truth. Shruti could never be recovered and one day she would have to let go of her mother. But is it easy to let go of your mother while she breathes and you take away her life?

Nidhi was lost in her thoughts when her phone buzzed. Nidhi received a message on her phone.

"Tomorrow at 9 am, don't get late on your first day – Reyaansh."

How did he get my phone number? Oh, he's my boss obviously he would have my phone number. Nidhi thought to herself.

"I'm never late. 9 it is. –Nidhi" Nidhi sent the message.

Within a fraction of minute, her phone buzzed again.

"You impressed me with your confidence. Let's see whether your work is as impressive as you –Reyaansh"

"Obviously you'll love my work because I'm different – Nidhi" Nidhi replied.

"And how exactly is that? –Reyaansh"

"I give my 102% rather than giving 100%. 2% extra for the work I love –Nidhi" Nidhi replied.

"You manage to amuse me very much. Hope you are this energetic tomorrow as well. Good Night. –Reyaansh"

How on earth do I amuse you anyway? Nidhi thought to herself.

"Good Night –Nidhi" Nidhi replied.

Nidhi kept the phone aside and walked out of the bed. She walked out of her room and descended the stairs. She walked to the balcony. It was a small balcony with plants covered all over. She looked up and she saw the moon and a billion stars or more. It was a beautiful sight. There was a thing about stars, she always fell in love with them; the moment she saw them. She leaned herself on the wall and relaxed. Wind caressed her cheek slowly.

There is something in Reyaansh which is very odd. Everything was very uncomfortable. Maybe I'm just judging him quite too quick. Perhaps, I should not judge him this soon. Maybe he's a good person and probably I'm over thinking. Naina thought to herself and sighed.

She looked at the moon. The moon is alone and still looks beautiful. And when, one looks at the sky, it looks like the stars just add the charm to the presence of the moon.

I should probably sleep else I'll be fired on day 1. Nidhi smiled and looked at the moon.

Nidhi reached the office at 8:45 am and waited in the cabin as she was instructed. She wore a red shirt tucked into black pencil skirt and medium-sized heels. She had her hair open this time but safeguarded with clips so that they don't fall on her face.

"You're before time, Miss Bhaweja." Reyaansh said.

Nidhi turned around to find Reyaansh. He looked at her and smiled.

"You look stunning. Red suits you." Reyaansh said and smiled.

"Thanks." Nidhi said.

"So ready for the work you love?"

"Always,"

Reyaansh smiled at Nidhi.

He elaborated the work to Nidhi. Her job, her work, her duties, all the rules and regulations to be followed, departmental rules and regulations, duties. Nidhi listened to him carefully asking him doubts and cross-questioning him. Reyaansh has never met such confident girl. She was communicating with him at such ease as if she knew him from a very long time. She was fearless and untamed and a very confident woman, the traits which Reyaansh loved the most. There have many people come into Reyaansh's life but none of them had the charm to make him stop and look upon the beauty in them, but Nidhi was an exception.

Nidhi met other employees, all the people who would be working under her, the important people and she was easily communicating with them. She was social which worked wonders for her. Nidhi went back to Reyaansh's office as he had called her. He asked her to assist him on some work and project related work. Nidhi helped him, explained a few things and gave him few suggestions and advices.

None of them realized while talking and sharing the work that a complete day passed by and it was evening already. They were so lost with completing the work.

"It's 5 in the evening. Let's pack up. We'll continue tomorrow." Reyaansh said.

"Yeah, I'm okay with it. I'll be there at 8:45." Nidhi said.

"I really like a person who takes work and time seriously."

Nidhi smiled.

"So what are you doing now? Going home?" Reyaansh asked.

"Well, probably not! I'm hungry so I'm going to grab a snack for myself from the canteen and then I'll go back." Nidhi said.

"I happen to feel hungry as well. Do you mind if I join you?"

Damn, why did I tell him that I'm hungry? Nidhi thought to herself.

"Umm…"

"There's a great restaurant I know, we can go there." Reyaansh said.

"Sir, I can't go to a restaurant in these clothes and…" Nidhi said making the dumbest excuse she could think of.

"Call me Reyaansh. And, we can buy you new clothes." Reyaansh said instantly.

"Sir… Reyaansh… I really don't think…"

"I treat you more like a friend and less like an employee and, trust me; you wouldn't want me treating you like an employee." Reyaansh said grinning.

What does that mean? Nidhi thought to herself.

"So, you want to go?"

Nidhi sighs slowly. *No options.* She thought to herself.

"Okay." Nidhi said.

"Good." Reyaansh smiled.

Nidhi forced a smile.

Nidhi and Reyaansh walked down to the car parking. There was a separate parking for Reyaansh. There was a black car parked. *Obviously, it had to be black. Is he color blind or something? Doesn't he know about the existence of other colors as well? This is strange.* Nidhi thought to herself.

CHAPTER-21

Nidhi wore a black dress and black heels which Reyaansh forced her completely to buy, she had her hair open. They were in a Thai and Chinese restaurant.

"So, Nidhi tell me about your parents." Reyaansh asked.

"My parents died when I was small, in a car crash. My aunt and grandmother took care of me ever since." Nidhi said.

"Oh, I'm sorry."

"What about you?"

"Even my parents died. Never saw my mother. Dad and an elder brother died leaving the industry on me. I only have one sister who studies in Europe. She's the only person left, and is, my only family." Reyaansh said and smiled.

Nidhi returned the smiled.

"Do you miss them?" Nidhi asked.

"Miss who?"

"Your parents,"

"Yes, I do very much, you?"

"Not much, but yes, I was very small when the accident took place."

"Oh so other than loving your job, what else you love?"

"Like my interests?"

"Yes."

"Writing and Travelling."

"I saw the writing part though. You're great."

"Thank you."

"What places have you visited?"

"Nowhere, to be honest,"

"So, traveling is your interests? How?" Reyaansh asks in confusion.

"It's like I've never been anywhere, that's why I have a thirst to visit places especially out of India." Nidhi smiled.

"Wow, that's amazing. So what will you eat?"

"Anything vegetarian please,"

"Okay. I accept just one thing from a person. Not more than one." Reyaansh grinned.

What does that mean? Nidhi thought to herself.

They ordered food and talked a lot. Reyaansh told Nidhi about his industry and told her incidents, his interviews and about the places he has visited in and out of India whereas Nidhi told him about the *tragic love story of Shruti and Armaan* when Reyaansh asked about her middle name. Reyaansh was a completely different person than Nidhi was. Maybe that's why Reyaansh was strongly attracted towards Nidhi.

After finishing the food, Nidhi insisted to split the bill but Reyaansh didn't accept. It was really awkward for Nidhi as Reyaansh was continuously spending a really huge amount of money on her even after her denials. They walked back to Reyaansh's black car, as he drove to Nidhi's house to drop her.

"9 in the morning don't be late." Reyaansh said.

"8:45 in the morning, I'm never late." Nidhi said.

"I love the way you speak, so confidently." Reyaansh said.

Nidhi smiled and got off from the car.

"Good night." Reyaansh said.

"Good Night." Nidhi said.

Nidhi walked back into her bungalow while Reyaansh went back to his home. Suchitra opened the door as soon as she hears the sound of car honks.

"It's so late where were you and what is all this? What are you wearing?" Suchitra asks out of concern.

Nidhi elaborates the whole story how Reyaansh wanted to accompany her to eat, as she was hungry and he took her to the restaurant and bought her clothes as she couldn't wear official clothes to a restaurant.

"Wow. I think Reyaansh is interested in you!" Suchitra says happily.

"I don't know but I don't really like him."

"Why? He looks good."

"What? Is physical appearance everything?" Nidhi asks.

"No, he's wealthy and he looks good." Suchitra says and laughs.

"It's not funny."

"Okay, but really. It does look like he has fallen in love with you."

"But I don't like him."

"Why?"

"There's something so off about Reyaansh. I mean negativity. As if he's hiding something. Something like he's not somebody he shows that he is." Nidhi said.

"Do you know you think so much? Maybe he's just sweet and showing his sweet gestures. See he's rich so he'll gift you things up to his standards. That's why he took you to the store and bought you clothes and took you to the restaurant because he can. That's the only reason. You're probably overthinking. Maybe he wants to be friends with you. Rich people have everything, but still are lonely to some extent. Maybe he found a friend in you."

Nidhi was speechless because she thought to what Suchitra said and listened carefully. Maybe Suchitra was right. Reyaansh has not said or done anything wrong he has always been kind to her. He always did help her when she was in need.

Maybe he really is a nice man. Nidhi thought to herself.

Nidhi walked back into her room as she finished her food. She tried to sleep to sleep but her mind kept on thinking.

Maybe he just wanted to be friends with me and I'm overthinking and taking all of this in a different way. Nidhi thought to herself. Nidhi accepted the fact that she was wrong and went to sleep.

~

The next morning Nidhi was before time as usual. It was a dry morning a Monday morning and everyone in the office was sleepy and tired mostly.

"Hi!" A girl said when she entered the office.

"Hey!" Nidhi said.

"I'm Maya and you're Nidhi, right?" Maya said and smiled.

"Wow, you know me?" Nidhi asked in surprise.

"Not only me! The whole office knows you." Maya said.

"What? How?" Nidhi says as they both walked inside to the waiting room.

"You're the daring girl who's working with Reyaansh Singhania, Nidhi. No one has ever dared to do that for many years." Maya said.

"What do you mean?" Nidhi asks.

"Well… He's very aggressive. He treats his employees so badly. But, I can see he doesn't treat you like that which is strange. You're lucky he doesn't do that. But take care of yourself." Maya said worryingly.

"Take care? What do you mean?" Nidhi asks out of concern.

Someone calls out for Maya from the corridor.

"Just, take care of yourself. People don't really last with Reyaansh. They basically disappear." Maya said and walked away towards the person who was calling out for her.

Till then, Reyaansh entered the office so Nidhi rushed inside his cabin to check whether everything was arranged or not.

"Good Morning, Nidhi." Reyaansh smiled.

"Morning, Sir." Nidhi wished back.

Reyaansh raised his eyebrows and Nidhi found it hilarious. She smiled.

"Sorry, I mean Reyaansh."

"Better."

They sat and talked a lot about Nidhi's first project which was really important for the Singhania Industries as well. Nidhi thought of herself as a friend, Reyaansh was looking, but the things Maya told to her kept running on her mind. But she didn't take her much seriously since the way Reyaansh talked to her, so casually and calmly, which was something so opposite to what she thought Reyaansh was and how Maya portrayed him as. Nidhi, in fact, thought of him as a very nice person.

"Reyaansh, I have something in my mind."

"Yes, go ahead." Reyaansh said.

"You did so many things for me, yesterday I mean. I'm thankful, and I wanted to return the favor."

"Friends don't return the favor, Nidhi. You're my friend and I love to please myself by pleasing the people I love."

Nidhi giggled, "That's really sweet of you Reyaansh but really. I wanted to invite you to dinner tonight."

"Dinner at your house?" Reyaansh asked.

"Yes. I won't take your answer as no. Friends don't take answers as no." Nidhi laughed.

"Besides everything is arranged as well, you have to come." Nidhi requested.

"Oh, Nidhi, I have my very important meeting tonight with the clients, about the project we're working on."

Nidhi frowns, "Oh."

Reyaansh picks up the receiver and dials a number.

"Hello, Nikita. Please cancel all the meetings for tonight I have something important tonight, thanks."

Nidhi's eyes were wide open and Reyaansh laughs.

"Why did you cancel your meeting?" Nidhi asks.

"Priorities," Reyaansh smiled.

Nidhi blushes.

It was in evening when Reyaansh arrived at Nidhi's home for dinner. As being a host, Nidhi left early from the office to do some work and help her grandmother too. She cleaned the house and helped Suchitra in making food. She switched on the radio to play some songs. It was almost the time for Reyaansh to come.

"You should go and change." Suchitra said.

"But I'm fine with what I'm wearing." Nidhi still was wearing work clothes- a skirt and a shirt.

"No, wear something else." Suchitra said scolding her.

Naina nodded since she had no choice. Nidhi walked inside into her room to change. After a while, the doorbell rang. Nidhi ran and peeked who was standing behind the door from the window. Reyaansh stood there, he held a bouquet of flowers in his hands and he was running his hand through his hair. Naina smirked. She opened the door. Reyaansh looked at her; she wore a white chikan kurta, with black palazzos. She had her hair open. Reyaansh kept looking at her with a smile. Nidhi blushed as she tucked her hair strands behind her ears and looked up back at him and smiled back. Suchitra walked towards the gate and greeted Reyaansh and welcomed him inside as he gave the bouquets to Suchitra.

"You have a beautiful house." Reyaansh said.

"Thank you; we tried our best to maintain the beauty of it. After our loss in business, mostly our staff left since we couldn't pay for their services but a few of them stayed with us out of loyalty." Suchitra smiled.

They all sat on the couch as a maid brought them sorbets. They all talked, Nidhi told how everyone loved her at the office whereas Reyaansh said it was because of her hard-work and willingness to work. They all went to the dining table as they ate their food after the maid and Suchitra served them food.

"So tell me Reyaansh about your family." Suchitra asked Reyaansh.

"I only have my sister who studies in Europe. I never saw my mother and my dad and brother died in an accident, ever since I'm taking care of our company." Reyaansh said.

"It must be so tragic for you and your sister. Losing everyone in such young years, how are you coping?" Suchitra asked.

"*I guess you never learn to recover from the incidents where you lose the people you love.*" Reyaansh said.

Nidhi looked at Reyaansh, his eyes looked empty. Nidhi could feel the pain because she could relate to the pain he was feeling. She felt it too. Nidhi placed her hands on Reyaansh's and said, "Don't worry everything will be fine." Perhaps it was a reflex, but she meant it. *When you lose someone you don't really move on from the pain of separation, you just slowly either get used to the pain or replace those feelings with other.*

Reyaansh looked at Nidhi smiled and nodded. They both almost forgot the presence of Suchitra, they felt cautious and when they looked at her she was just smiling. After completing the dinner Reyaansh said that he should be leaving now. The songs still were playing on the radio all this time while he was in Nidhi's home. Nidhi walked him to the front door. Reyaansh stopped and looked back at her.

"You look beautiful, if it isn't quite too obvious." Reyaansh smiled and looked at her.

Nidhi blushed and tucked her hair strands behind her ears and looked up at him.

"Thanks for coming today." Nidhi said and smiled.

"I like spending my time with you, Nidhi." Reyaansh smiled and looked at Naina.

Naina smiled like a small kid. She had no idea what to say. *Sometimes we hear or read things which struck us straight into our heart. Something so beautiful that you feel it's warmth in your heart, you feel the warmth in your cheeks as you blush crimson. But your lips quiet, it wants to say something but its gets all caught up. That's why we get speechless.* That's why Nidhi was left speechless.

"Reyaansh," Nidhi says.

"Yeah,"

"You are a really nice man." Nidhi smiled.

Reyaansh smiled back. He walked out of the door as Nidhi watched him go back into his car. Nidhi closed the door and smiled again.

I was so wrong, I have been wrong all these time damn. He is so sweet and he's such an amazing person. Nidhi thought to herself and smiled more. As the radio played songs, she noticed the song's lyrics.

Aye mere dil Mubarak ho, yahi to pyaar hai

Ishq Mubarak.

Nidhi smiled even more as she blushed.

Reyaansh and Nidhi started to spend the most of the time with each other. Suchitra also liked Reyaansh a lot. Reyaansh was falling in love deeper and deeper with every passing day. He spent most of his money on her even after her denials. Within a week, Nidhi got a promotion as well.

Nidhi was completely happy. Slowly, Nidhi fell in love with Reyaansh as well as Suchitra also encouraged Reyaansh's feelings for Nidhi. Reyaansh used to live alone and when he asked her to move in, she accepted. Everything was beautiful like a fantasy world she was living in and she couldn't be any happier. Sometimes Reyaansh used to scream and shout at her when they had a fight. But then, she thought it's completely healthy in a relationship because when they had a fight and Reyaansh used to treat her badly, but he also felt guilty and he used to make it up to her. He then used to take her out or cook for her. She soon realized that Maya was right in some terms. He really was short-tempered and very aggressive. But he was madly in love with Nidhi.

She thought whether the other things which Maya mentioned were true or not, or what if they happen to be true? But when Reyaansh proposed Nidhi, she said a yes. They were finally engaged and, the thought about all the things that Maya told her and the negative thoughts faded.

Reyaansh and Nidhi confessed their obvious feelings to Suchitra, that they loved each other and wanted to get married. Suchitra always liked Reyaansh. She thought that Reyaansh was a successful man and can keep Nidhi happy. She thought he can give all the happiness that she always lacked in. Nidhi and Suchitra wanted a proper wedding ceremony but Reyaansh wanted a court marriage but, after a lot of discussion and arguments and fights, Nidhi and Suchitra had to obey to Reyaansh.

Finally, Reyaansh and Nidhi got married to each other.

CHAPTER-22

Reyaansh and Nidhi were happy for the first two to three days after when Nidhi slowly started to find out what kind of a guy Reyaansh really was. Reyaansh started to open up to what he actually was. Reyaansh fired all the servants from his bungalow so that he could get privacy with Nidhi. But, that turned out to be the biggest challenge in Nidhi's life.

Reyaansh gave all the duties of the servants to Nidhi. Nidhi was no longer allowed to work. When she asked the reason behind it, Reyaansh simply said you're my wife. We are already wealthy enough to afford any lifestyle, so there's no need for Nidhi to work and when she insisted to work, Reyaansh slapped her and said never to force him with things. It was the first time he slapped her, raised his hand on her. She thought it was okay as it's the first time and it'll be the last time. He was her husband now; she thought it gives him the authority to do so. After all, Nidhi loved Reyaansh. She thought that it was okay if Reyaansh scolded her. *Even today there are many women who stay quiet when their husband or boyfriends raises their hands not to love their wife or girlfriends but to beat them. They think it's perfectly normal. Is it? Is it okay for your 'better half' to hit you? You see, when we are in love, we would never want to reflect any kind of hurt or pain to the ones we love. And if they hit you, it's surely not love.*

She had no choice but to listen to Reyaansh. She had to make sure if all the things were cleaned and dust free and all the things were kept in order. Even if one thing was wrong, Reyaansh used to scold her and slapped her. And soon, the beating her became a habit of Reyaansh; sometimes a necessity to take out his frustrations and anger or sometimes just for entertainment. Slowly, Nidhi stopped speaking much, the way she used to. She changed. *From a beautiful flower, she became a slowly dying rose.*

"Nidhi, I'm back," Reyaansh came back.

Nidhi panics when she hears Reyaansh's voice.

Nidhi came running with a glass of water in the tray.

"I'm so sorry I was cleaning and I forgot to keep the glass on the table." Nidhi said.

Reyaansh looks at her, smiles. He picks up the glass and throws the water on her face.

"I married you because you were so good with time and your work. What happened to that energy of you? Next time bring the glass on time."

"You can't treat me like this, Reyaansh!" She said in a small voice.

"Oh? You'll teach me now how to treat a woman?"

"Yes, I will because no one ever taught you." She said accumulating a little strength.

"What if I don't listen to you? What can you do?" Reyaansh laughs.

"I'm going back to my home. I can't resist your tortures anymore." Nidhi shouts.

Reyaansh stretches his arms and slaps Nidhi so hard that she fell and the glass fell on the ground as well. A piece of glass cuts inside her skin making her blood spill out.

"Oh god! Nidhi, look what you made me do. Are you okay baby?" Reyaansh said.

Reyaansh helps Nidhi to stand up. Reyaansh's hand left an imprint on her cheeks. He looks at it. He leans in towards Nidhi. Nidhi was already crying while he kissed her cheeks making her feel the pain more than before. He takes out the piece of the glass and takes her hand to his mouth and sucks all the blood.

"You're mine, Nidhi. If you ever, even think of going back, I'll not kill you, darling."

Nidhi looks at him with a little hope.

"I'll kill everyone in your house." Reyaansh looked at Nidhi and smiled.

"Now go and get ready. Let's go out to that restaurant where we went for our first date." Reyaansh said.

Nidhi managed herself to get herself cleaned. She was scared of the things he just said. It was the first time he hit her this bad. She thought it'll be the last. She was wrong again. In the evening, they went to the same restaurant.

"What would you like to have baby?" Reyaansh asked.

"Anything," Nidhi shivers.

Reyaansh called out the waiter and ordered food containing chicken.

"Reyaansh, I'm pure vegetarian." Nidhi said in a low voice.

Reyaansh stopped speaking with the waiter, he looked at Naina.

"Baby, why do you always interrupt me?"

Reyaansh looked at the waiter, "Add chocolate truffle pastries as well. That'll be all."

"Get up," Reyaansh said looking at Nidhi.

Nidhi gets up.

"Serve water to me,"

Nidhi pours water into the glass to gives it to Reyaansh.

He drinks and spits the water on Nidhi's face.

"Why do you get me angry?" Reyaansh shouts.

People around the table started to look at them.

"Go and sit now," Reyaansh said.

Nidhi agrees with him and sits down.

The manager of the restaurant came to their table and asks Nidhi whether everything was okay. Nidhi smiles and says yes everything's okay.

"Actually yes, there is a problem. I really feel so hot in here. Can you please decrease the ac temperature?"

"But..." The manager said in shock.

"Do as you're being told. You know who I am and what I can do right?" Reyaansh said.

"Okay." The manager said giving a sorry expression to Nidhi.

The waiter brings food. He keeps it on the table and serves the food for both of them.

Reyaansh begins to eat and asks her to eat as well.

"What happened, baby?" Reyaansh asked.

"N… Nothing,"

"Didn't you like the dishes?" Reyaansh asked again.

Nidhi doesn't speak.

"Nidhi, darling, tell me what it is. I'm sure you don't want to see me angry out here in public. Right?"

"I can't eat anything non-vegetarian." Nidhi managed to say.

"I don't like investing my money in things I don't like Nidhi. And, I don't like vegetarian food." Reyaansh smiled.

Nidhi was blank.

"Eat." He shouted.

~

When they came back to home Nidhi had vomited thrice. She still was feeling sick and cold.

"I'm sorry, Nidhi. I shouldn't have asked you to eat chicken. You're not used to it." Reyaansh said being sorry.

"It's okay."

"No, I want to correct my mistake. I'll make you get used to it so you don't get any problem in eating non-vegetarian food." Reyaansh said.

Nidhi was blank.

"I'm going out for an official work for 5 days. I'll leave my chef to make you my favorite non-vegetarian dishes. You can starve or you can eat." Reyaansh said and smiled.

He locked the house and disconnected the telephone wires before leaving. Nidhi tries to run away but the only way to escape was the main gate which was locked. Nidhi starved herself for 2 days. But the third day, hunger won over her preferences. She ate the food and felt disgusted and she vomited again. The next day again, she felt disgusted but didn't vomit. The fifth day, she ate it without any problems. Reyaansh took over the charm of Nidhi and she lost herself completely. When he came he celebrated his victory by drinking whiskey.

She couldn't take any more. She had bruises and marks all over her body. Reyaansh had started now beating her more badly and using his leather belt to beat her. She was in a pathetic condition. She had no other choice but to do what he says to avoid the punishments. But, her soul was on fire. She decided to take the advantage of the night and to run away. She thought she can run away back to her grand-mother, to Suchitra. They will make her feel safe again. Even the old cook felt so sorry for Nidhi's condition when she told her the truth and begged her to help her out. The cook decided to help her run away.

Reyaansh slept early that day because the old cook mixed sleeping pill in his drink. Nidhi took out the key of the main door from his pocket.

"I wish you were the person I thought you were, Reyaansh. I really loved you. But, I'll not accept the things you do to me. I'm sorry." Nidhi said.

She wiped her tears and thanked the old cook for helping her out and, somehow successfully escaped.

She ran outside the bungalow. She turned back to see the last time Reyaansh's house, moreover a house she was imprisoned. It was black in color just like Reyaansh's heart. It had huge glass windows and curtains and there was a swimming pool in front of it and a parking lot and an entrance beside it. It was the kind of a house anyone would die to have. But for Nidhi, it was a house where she *died every day*, but not anymore.

She ran down the main road and took a taxi to go back to her home. She was finally free and tears of joy cascade her cheeks as a smile run down her lips. She was finally free from that torture house and could return to her family again. She just wanted to keep her head on her mother's lap and cry her heart out.

When the taxi reached its destination, she gave the driver money which the old cook gave her to use whenever she would in need of. She'll always be thankful of her. She ran inside to find something which broke her completely.

She saw the bungalow on fire. She screamed out loud. She ran to save her family, her mother and her grandmother when someone grabbed her hand from behind.

"You think you're smarter?" Reyaansh laughed.

"That's what I love the most about you. You think you're winning but, I never learned how to lose." Reyaansh kept laughing.

183

"Let go off me, I need to save them." Nidhi screamed.

"Baby, you need to understand. I get the things I want, one way or the other." Reyaansh said.

"You think I didn't know about your little plan of escaping? I heard your conversation between the cook and you. You seriously think my servants would ever disobey me? They've seen the worse of me. These all things are just a starter pack for you." Reyaansh said.

"Leave me please, I beg." Nidhi cried.

"I told you already. If you try to go back, I'll kill everyone you love. Do you really think anyone would be alive till now?"

Nidhi kept struggling for her freedom while Reyaansh enjoyed it.

"Oh, Nidhi do you know how happy you make me. Now it'll be just you and me, forever." Reyaansh said and laughed.

CHAPTER-23

After 2 years of continuous torture, abuses and getting beaten up by belts. Nidhi mentally died. She couldn't resist the fact that she had no one. She had no one she could go to and share what she feels. She wanted to cry her heart out but her tears went dry and she was tired. Her soul was tired. She was living with a person who killed her mother, who killed her grandmother. She was living with a murderer. It was a constant mental torturer. She somehow thought it was her destiny.

Suddenly the doorbell rings. Nidhi walks to the main gate and opens the door. There was a young girl standing with her suitcases. As soon as she saw Nidhi a huge smile comes on her face.

"Oh my god, Nidhi!" The girl shouted.

"Yes, who are you?" Nidhi asked.

"What you don't know me?" The girl entered the house.

"Wait, who are you? And why are you entering without permission?" Nidhi exclaimed.

"She doesn't need a permission to enter my house Nidhi." Reyaansh said descending the stairs.

"Reyaansh!" The girl screamed out loud and ran to and hugged Reyaansh tightly.

"Zoya! What a surprise, darling! I'm so happy to see you." Reyaansh said.

"Nidhi this is Zoya, my sister, I told you about." Reyaansh said pulling away Zoya from his hug.

"Oh! Hello." Nidhi said with a small smile on her face.

"I'm so sorry I couldn't make it to your wedding." Zoya said.

"Oh it's okay it was a private affair. Not much people came to the wedding." Reyaansh said.

"Oh." Zoya said.

"Now that you're here, you're not leaving for a month!" Reyaansh said.

"I'm actually here to stay." Zoya said.

"Obviously," Reyaansh laughed.

"No, you don't understand, Reyaansh. I'm here to apply for my college admissions." Zoya said.

"Why do you want to do a graduation in India, Zoya? When you can easily get your degree from any high-class college you want to in Europe or America."

"I don't want to stay away from home, Reyaansh after what happened to Mom, Dad, and Rehmaan." Zoya said.

"I miss my brother. I don't want to stay away from you. You're my only family." Zoya says as tears fell from her cheeks.

Reyaansh hugs her tight.

"I don't like my Zoya crying okay? I hate it when you cry. You want to live with us, you will live with us." Reyaansh said.

"Thanks." Zoya said wiping away her tears.

"It's okay. What happened in past, let it stay in the past. You and I will make your future worth living. Okay?" Reyaansh said.

"You always were my favorite brother!" Zoya laughed.

"I just love when you say this." Reyaansh laughed.

"Okay, you should go and rest. I have a meeting so I'll be back in the evening then we'll talk a lot. Okay?" Reyaansh said.

"Yes. Bye, Reyaansh" Zoya waved Reyaansh goodbye.

"Bye." Reyaansh waved her back and walked towards Nidhi.

Reyaansh hugged Nidhi and leaned towards her ears.

"Take good care of my sister and if you tell her anything, you know the consequences." Reyaansh whispered.

Nidhi nodded in acceptance and Reyaansh walked out of the house.

Zoya dragged her suitcase inside and rested on the couch while Nidhi brought her a glass of water.

"Thank you, Nidhi. So how are you?" Zoya asked.

"I'm good." Nidhi said as she sat beside her.

"So how was the wedding? I bet it was love marriage! I don't know many details so pardon me for that. I haven't been in touch with Reyaansh lately." Zoya said and smiled.

Nidhi sighed slowly. It reminded her of all the things she went through. She remembered how happy she was on the starting, when her job started in the office, when she was with her grandmother and her mother. But she took one misinterpreted a man. A man she thought to be as a gentleman, who is suffering from pain was actually a demon waiting to unleash. From losing her family to losing herself, it all happened from one wrong step-Marrying Reyaansh.

"It was good, as well." Nidhi lied.

"Okay, I'd like to rest for a while now." Zoya said and smiled. She got up.

"Wait. What would you like to have for dinner?" Nidhi stumbled.

"Anything," Zoya smiled and walked towards her room.

Zoya entered her room and the memories of the past, all the good and the bad. She wanted to savor all the happy memories in solitude.

~

"The food is delicious. It's just you should've added a little more salt to it." Zoya smiled at Nidhi.

The three of them were on the dining table as Nidhi served Reyaansh and Zoya food. The dining room was huge and was in a separate room near to kitchen. The table was long, with an antique Romanian candle stand at the center and a silver chandelier above it.

"I'm so sorry, Please forgive me. I didn't mean to do it I swear to god, I…" Nidhi stumbled.

"It's okay darling, we'll see what we should do about this mistake later." Reyaansh smiled and interrupted.

"What mistake? It's okay. It happens. Can you pass me the salt please?" Zoya laughed.

"Y… Yes." Nidhi stumbled again.

"It's okay, Nidhi. The food is delicious anyway!" Zoya smiled.

"Thanks." Nidhi forced a smile after when Reyaansh gave her a stern look.

"Why don't you join us?" Zoya asked.

"Indian values and ethics, Zoya. She cannot eat before I do." Reyaansh said.

Zoya looked at Nidhi, "Oh come-on. Don't be so old-fashioned. Eat with us."

"No, it's okay. I'll eat later." Nidhi smiled.

After finishing the food, Zoya excused herself as she was very tired and wanted to sleep. She wished Reyaansh and Nidhi goodnight and left.

"Why don't you go and make me something in the desert?" Reyaansh looked at Nidhi and smiled.

"But I already made…" Nidhi stopped when Reyaansh frowned.

"Okay." Nidhi said.

"Wise decision," Reyaansh smiled again.

Nidhi walked to the kitchen, while Reyaansh followed. Nidhi collected all the ingredients which were necessary for her dessert. As soon as she opened the stove, Reyaansh grabbed her palm of hands and placed over it.

Nidhi screamed.

Reyaansh slapped her and moved her palm closer to the flame.

"The more you scream, the closer your palm goes." Reyaansh said as he kissed Nidhi's cheeks.

Nidhi pressed her lips tightly and started biting it as tears rushed out of her eyes. She tried her best not to scream.

"Good girl. I like how you have started to listen to me." Reyaansh said as he moved her hand away from the flame.

"Why was the salt so less in the food?" Reyaansh whispered in her ears.

Naina doesn't reply.

"I don't like when people ignore me, baby." Reyaansh again moved her hands towards the stove.

"I'm sorry, I'm sorry. I didn't mean to." Nidhi cried.

"Does it take a lot to take care of my sister?" Reyaansh asked moving her hands away from the stove.

"No. The mistake won't be repeated. I'll take good care of her." Nidhi sobbed.

"You better do." Reyaansh left her hands.

Nidhi sobbed harder as she looked at her hands. They were burnt so badly.

"Oh my god, Nidhi! Your hand is burnt so badly. Look what you made me do." Reyaansh said and frowned.

He goes out of the kitchen while Nidhi tried not to cry. Reyaansh returned with a first aid kit. He applied ointment and covers her hand in bandages.

"Now using this hand Nidhi please make some dessert for me." Reyaansh smiled.

Nidhi was so shocked to hear.

What kind of a monster is her? She thought to herself and sobbed.

"The pain would anyway remind you not to forget sugar in my dessert." Reyaansh mocked and laughed.

CHAPTER-24

"Good Morning, Zoya!" Reyaansh smiled at Zoya while she came out from her room into the living room.

"Good Morning." Zoya greeted back.

"Are you okay? You look like you didn't sleep last night." Reyaansh said.

"No, I'm alright. It's just the different time zone thing." Zoya said.

"It's okay, you'll get used to it." Reyaansh said.

"Where's Nidhi?" Zoya asked?

"Cooking breakfast," Reyaansh said.

"What about all the servants?" Zoya asked.

"I fired them all because I needed privacy after our marriage." Reyaansh laughed.

Zoya smiled softly. "I'll be back in a minute. I should go and see if she needs help." Zoya stands up.

"Why would she? She can handle it all alone. Don't bother much." Reyaansh gives a stern look.

Suddenly Nidhi comes. "Breakfast is ready." She forces a smile.

Zoya notices Nidhi's injured hand and instantly looks at Nidhi.

"Let's go, then." Reyaansh said.

They all walk to the table while Nidhi serves them breakfast.

"Zoya, is the amount of salt in the food, okay today?" Reyaansh asks seriously.

"Yes, it's perfectly fine," Zoya replied.

"Okay. I have to go to the office. I shall take my leave now. I'll see you both in the evening." Reyaansh said.

Reyaansh hugs Nidhi. "Good girl." He kisses Nidhi's cheeks. "Bye." Reyaansh says.

"Bye." Nidhi forces a smile again.

Reyaansh smiles at Zoya and she smiles back, and he leaves as Nidhi closes the door.

"Nidhi," Zoya calls out her name.

Nidhi walks back to the dining table as she heard Zoya calling her name. She saw Zoya standing. Zoya runs and hugs her tightly. Zoya was crying.

"What's wrong?" Nidhi asks.

"I'm so sorry, I…" Zoya stumbled.

"Why are you saying sorry, Zoya? What happened?" Nidhi asks worryingly as she wiped Zoya's tears from her injured hands.

"This." Zoya touches Nidhi's hands softly.

Nidhi hesitates. "I... this actually... I..."

"I saw what happened last night, Nidhi. What Reyaansh did to you," Zoya cried.

Nidhi didn't say anything.

"It all happened because of me. I'm so sorry, Nidhi." Zoya cried harder.

"Shh! don't cry, Zoya." Nidhi hugs her.

"I'm okay, I swear." Nidhi said.

"No, you're not!" Zoya screams.

"Reyaansh is so inhuman! I know what things he is capable of. I shouldn't have said such things, I'm so sorry!"

"Zoya, it's okay. I'm really okay. Everything's fine." Nidhi hugs her tightly.

Nidhi hugs her tightly and doesn't let her go till she stopped crying. She brought a glass of water for her and made her sit on the chair. Nidhi sat beside her.

"You know I can easily catch people lying. I know you're not okay. I know how he is. I've seen him ever since we all were kids."

Nidhi doesn't say anything.

"I can see the bruises and injuries on your body, Nidhi. And, after what happened last night, I'm not a fool." Zoya said.

"I don't know what you're ta-talking about." Nidhi stammered.

"I never treated him like my brother"

Nidhi gave a stern look at Zoya.

"Yes, Nidhi, I don't treat him like my brother and I never will. I just pretend because I know how he can be."

"Why?"

"He never treated us as a family. I don't know how he has affectionate feelings for me. Maybe they're fake."

"What did he do to you?" Nidhi asked.

"I was a baby when my mom and dad adopted Reyaansh. Mom died soon after then. We always treated Reyaansh as our brother, and as I grew up I used to stay very scared of Reyaansh. I knew he was very short tempered. Our elder brother Rehmaan, he loved Reyaansh very much and used to tell me there's nothing to be afraid of him. Dad grew us up. He never discriminated in between us. He treated us all equally. But when I came to know that he was adopted, I never treated him as my brother. Dad sent me to London for my high-school and further studies. And, then dad died. That changed everything. I came back. When the time came for who will take over the company, Dad's power of attorney said that everything after him would equally divide into his three kids. But the company would belong to Rehmaan. It was just the next day, Nidhi. At night, I was walking to my room when I myself saw Reyaansh stabbing Rehmaan with a knife. Not only this, he confessed that he murdered dad to take over the company. I knew he would kill me if I stayed any longer. I booked my flight and went back. I was scared because I was young; I had nightmares and needed treatments for a long time.

Nidhi, I know how he is."

Nidhi cried listening to everything Zoya said. Nidhi confessed to all the torture Reyaansh has been doing. How he killed her family in front of her eyes. Nidhi couldn't believe that all this while she has been thinking that the pain has shaped him into such a demon. That his mother and father died then his brother died who he loved so much, probably that is why he's the way he is. *Probably you cannot justify for everyone's behavior, sometimes it's just the way they are.*

"I don't know what to say."

"I know, Nidhi. He's a monster."

"He is." Nidhi sighed.

"You don't have to worry now."

"What do you mean?"

"I'm here now, Nidhi." Zoya held her hands and wiped her tears.

"No one can hurt you now." She completed.

"I don't understand, Zoya. What do you have in your mind?"

"I have something cool." Zoya said.

"What?" Nidhi sobbed.

"A plan," Zoya said.

"A plan?"

"Yes."

"It's Reyaansh we're talking about, Zoya." Nidhi said.

"I know, Reyaansh. And I've known him longer than you know him." Zoya said.

"See, I know how his mind works and at what extent he can think." Zoya added.

"But what plan do you have?" Nidhi asked.

"Don't worry, he likes to play games, we'll play it way better than him." Zoya smiled.

"Zoya you do know that if it goes wrong, you'll put yourself in danger."

"I know that, but he needs to be stopped, Nidhi. And you need to be set free." Zoya said.

"Enough is enough; no one can treat women this way. No man has a right to ill-treat a woman, beat her or make her feel this pathetic, vulnerable. Nidhi you are stronger than you think you are. You have been fighting this from the past so many years and you have nothing to lose. *And when people have nothing to lose they become undefeatable and unbreakable.*"

Nidhi listened to Zoya in silence.

"Nidhi, say something,"

"I don't know what to say."

"Nidhi, either you can back off and tolerate Reyaansh's torture or fight today and enjoy your freedom tomorrow and forever." Zoya said.

Nidhi sighed.

"So are you with me?"

"Yes." Nidhi said.

"But what's the plan?" Nidhi asked.

CHAPTER-25

Nidhi started packing her bag as Zoya helped. Everything happened all of a sudden. But it was important for Nidhi to run away. She had no choice.

"Where will I go, Zoya?" Nidhi asked.

"Delhi." Zoya said, helping her packing.

"How will I go?"

"You'll go by bus ok?"

"The last time I tried to escape, I lost my family."

"What do you have now to lose? You've nearly lost yourself! It's better to die than to live in this hell."

"I'm scared, Zoya."

Zoya hugged her. "You've seen so much, Nidhi. You've been through so much. You don't deserve such life. Nobody does. Nidhi, do this for yourself. Don't be scared. Everything will be okay."

"What will I do if Reyaansh caught me?" Nidhi stammered.

"He won't Nidhi, but if we won't hurry I'm sure he will!"

Nidhi nodded.

It was evening and the sun was about to set. The sky turned red from blue and the birds were returning home. And so was Nidhi. She was all packed up and was ready to leave.

"Nidhi, take some money. You'll be in need of them. Rent a flat in Delhi and get yourself a job. It'll help you. Take this phone; it has my phone number, emergency numbers on speed dials. Take care, okay?" Zoya said.

"Thank you so much, Zoya I can't explain how thankful I am." Nidhi sobbed.

Zoya hugged her, "Don't thank me Nidhi, you don't deserve this."

Nidhi hugged her back, "What about you? What if he finds out you helped me run away?"

"Nothing will happen, Nidhi." Zoya said. "You must go now." She finished.

"Yes." Nidhi hugged Zoya for the last time and walked towards the main gate.

She opened the gate to find Reyaansh standing.

As soon as Nidhi saw Reyaansh standing, her bag fell to the ground. Reyaansh noticed the bag.

"Going somewhere, love?" Reyaansh smiles wickedly.

"Reyaansh it was my bag." Zoya says.

Reyaansh walks inside grabbing Nidhi's wrist tightly.

"Those clothes were old so we thought we should go out to distribute those clothes to the beggars." Zoya smiled.

"Oh!" Reyaansh smiled back and eased up. He loosened his tight grip on Nidhi's hands.

"You should've told me that darling." Reyaansh smiled at Nidhi.

"Sorry." Nidhi forced a smile.

"I'll go and get fresh then I'd like to talk to you." Reyaansh smiled and said to Nidhi.

"Okay." Nidhi said.

Reyaansh starts to walk further he turns around and looks at Nidhi, "Are you willing to come by yourself or want to be forced to come?" Reyaansh laughed.

Reyaansh was standing in front of Zoya with his back faced. Zoya taking advantage of the situation grabbed a glass flower vase and she hit it on Reyaansh's head. Reyaansh screamed and Blood spilled out from his head, he placed his both hands on his head in pain and turned around taking a glimpse of Zoya he fell down to the ground.

"Why, Zoya?" Reyaansh said in pain and fainted.

Nidhi looked at Zoya instantly.

"What? Don't give me that look. I saw the vase, and I saw his head. The vase wanted to kiss Reyaansh's head. So I did what the vase wanted me to do." Zoya laughed.

"What if he dies?" Nidhi asked.

"He doesn't deserve to live either."

"But…"

"Nidhi, you need to go. Take care of yourself." Zoya said.

"Thank you." Nidhi said, and left.

"And, Nidhi please go to a doctor as well."

After a very long time, Nidhi literally smiled. She nodded in agreement.

CHAPTER-26

(PRESENT)

It was 5 am in the morning. The sun was about to rise. The sky turned from dark blue, to pink, to light blue. The sunlight touched the clouds and the mountains in Manali. One could witness the snow on the mountains sitting from their houses. The birds were chirping and the slow wind was blowing. It was a magical view. Away from the city, the traffic one could find their comfort in the silence in the hills of Manali.

That's what Vivaan and Naina did. *They found their solace in the silence. With time people only realize that the loudest cries are the ones which cannot be heard but felt. A situation which leaves you numb, just still. You freeze and your heart feels lifeless. Like you turn blank and you have absolutely no control over anything. At this point, no advice, no consolation, works but the one thing that redeems is one face, one touch, or one word from a right person.*

"Is Nidhi…?" Vivaan stammered.

"I'm Nidhi Arti Singhania, Vivaan."

Vivaan couldn't speak a thing. He was speechless but couldn't stop looking at Naina.

"Vivaan, it's not easy for someone like me to fall in love, to trust a person again." She chokes but manages to continue, "Vivaan, *I've been through so much and I'm hurt to that extinct that I can't really move on from the fear, and the sleepless nights. I don't know if I can ever move on from those wounds which are still fresh or the scars on every part of my body.*" Naina said.

Naina walked towards Vivaan. She wiped her tears and as well as Vivaan's. She stretched her hands and caresses both of his hands.

"You asked me whether I loved you or not?" Naina said slowly.

Vivaan and Naina's eyes met.

"Vivaan it's not easy for a girl like me to fall in love…"

"Do you remember when we were in the garden and you said you don't believe in love either? *Do you know when someone says they do not believe in love it simply means they do not trust love. They do not trust anyone else with their heart; they don't trust someone with their life…*"

"I trusted someone with love, I trusted someone with my heart and married him…"

"All I got was a broken heart, bruises and scars all over my body with broken bones, dead family…" Naina choked again as she tried to breathe in.

"Vivaan, with all these broken pieces of my heart and the scars, *I'm in love*" Naina choked again.

She breathes in heavily. "*I'm in love with you*, Vivaan."

Tears fell down from Vivaan's eyes.

"Can you love a girl who is not a whole? After knowing my truth, can you love me back?" Naina asked.

Vivaan doesn't say a word. It was the very first time that the silence between them was killing her.

"Vivaan," She said.

"Naina,"

"Say something, please." Naina said slowly.

Vivaan didn't say anything. Naina walks closer to Vivaan and she tries to hold his hands again, Vivaan took a step back.

"It's time to leave back for Delhi." Vivaan said without looking at Naina.

He took a step away from Naina and walked back inside the room. He left Naina standing alone. She sat on the chair and sighed deeply. She wiped her tears and looked at the garden as the swings were swinging by the wind.

Maybe I don't deserve love. Naina thought to herself.

CHAPTER-27

It was the month of autumn. The leaves shed from the trees and fell the ground. The wind blew and took the leaves away. The ground was covered in red and yellow colored dry leaves. It was cold but bearable. The wind was soothing. It was evening; the sun has already given its place to the moon. It was a full moon night.

Everyone came back to Delhi. None of them talked in the journey. Even, Sharara knew something happened and it was best to keep her quiet. Later after reaching to Delhi, they all traveled back to Vivaan's place. Vivaan's mother welcomed everyone back home as everyone walked inside.

"How was it?" Vivaan's mother smiled.

"Good." Vivaan replied and walked inside his room.

Vivaan's mother sensed something was wrong with him. She told everyone that the dinner was ready and Vivaan, Naina, and Sharara walked to the dinner table ate their meal. Later she asked Naina to sleep over their house since it was very late and to go back tomorrow. She accepted.

"Are you going to leave us?" Sharara asked

Sharara and Naina were in Sharara's room. Naina looked out from the window. She was blank as she didn't know what to say or how to explain things to her. She didn't know how Vivaan would react to the truth about her past, whether he would still like to see her or not. She neither wanted to give her any false hoped nor could she tell her the truth. She didn't know what to say.

"Please don't leave me!" Sharara began to weep.

"She's not going anywhere, Sharara." Vivaan said who was standing at the door listening to their conversation.

Sharara nodded and hugged Naina tightly. Naina kissed her forehead and asked her to sleep. Sharara nodded. Naina caressed her forehead as she slept like a small baby with no worries.

Vivaan walked to Naina and he clasped her hands softly. They walked out of the room to Vivaan's room.

"Naina,"

"Vivaan,"

"You told me about your past. You shared your pain, your scars. You told me everything. I couldn't believe that you went through so much, Naina. I just couldn't. And even after so much happened to you, you were so brave to fall in love with me. If I were you, I don't even know…" Vivaan sobbed.

Naina hugged him tightly. The touch was soft. They were hugged to each other for so long that Naina could live in those moments forever as if she was longing for a loving hug.

"Naina," Vivaan choked. He cleared his throat. "*You asked me if I could love a person like you. You asked if I could love a person that is not whole.*" Vivaan sobbed. Vivaan took Naina's hands into his as if he was holding it for the last time.

"I know it's hard for you, Naina. Trusting someone again like you did back then, loving someone again. It's hard and I know it! I know you've been brutally broken but you still had the courage to not deny its existence, to accept love, to accept me. You deserve a love deeper than the ocean. Naina, I'll pick your scars, I'll choose your pain rather than picking someone else's rainbows any day." Vivaan sobbed harder.

Naina was crying with him.

"I love you, Naina. I want to marry you." Vivaan said. He took out bangles from his pockets.

Naina looked at them in shock.

"These are my mother's. She likes you too." Vivaan giggled while crying.

"But why, Vivaan, even after knowing, my past, why do you love me?" Naina choked.

"Because you are like the moon, which is not only beautiful when full but also is beautiful in all of your phases and fractions and white broken pieces, I love you. I want to love you where your demons reside and all the scars you hide. I want to love you so intensely that you'll be left with no choice, but to heal. I want to love you so passionately that love- becomes the only emotion you'll be aware of and heartbreak becomes fictional to you. "

"I love you." Tears busted out of her eyes.

"I love you so much!" Vivaan said.

Vivaan hugged Naina tightly. He tucked the strands of her hair behind her ears. Her cheeks were wet. They were standing so close to each other. Naina could feel his breaths on her face. Vivaan leaned in and kissed the tears on her cheeks. Naina closed her eyes. He kissed her forehead. He kissed her nose. He slipped his hands behind her neck.

Naina's breaths quickened and Vivaan could feel all of it. He caressed her face with other hand and brought her face near to his. Naina's lips were soft and moist. He kissed her upper lips and the kissed her lower lips. Then their tongue met and intertwined. They kissed.

"...*I can forget my very existence when I kiss you.*" Vivaan said taking a minute to breathe and smiled.

They kissed slowly at first and then *they were kissing like drowning people breathe.* Vivaan brought his palm of his hands to her front neck as they kissed intensely.

He pushed her back on the wall as he grabbed both of her hands gently as he kept on kissing Naina without giving her a moment to breathe. He lifted her hands up while holding her hands, as he slowly went down kissing her neck. Naina hair her eyes close as she felt the two lips exploring every inch of her skin. Vivaan released her one hand as he ran his fingers on her neck. He started biting her neck and then he licked it. Vivaan started running his finders down her neck now. Naina held his neck with one hand and brought his face closer to his. She kissed his lips and his eyes.

"Vivaan,"

"Naina," Vivaan said as he looked into his eyes.

"Vivaan I need to tell you something." Naina said as she released her second hand and walked past him and stood a little away from him.

"Is everything okay?"

"Vivaan I can't do it."

"It's okay Naina, if you're not ready for it, we don't have to do it." Vivaan smiled and walked closer to her. He cupped her face with his hands as he kissed her forehead.

"I love you, you know that right?" Vivaan smiled.

"It's not that I'm not ready or something, it's just…" Naina choked.

"Then what is it, Naina?" Vivaan said worryingly.

"I'm not very proud of my skin, Vivaan. I'm not beautiful; I'm insecure of my skin. I have burns and bruises, the ugliest ones, I…" Naina choked.

"Naina, to me you're the most beautiful woman I've ever seen or will ever see. I don't care about anything else. You love me; this is the most important thing to me." Vivaan said.

"You don't understand, Vivaan." Naina said.

Vivaan kissed her eyes, "I do understand you are insecure about your body, perhaps every girl is. But if a man cannot love a lady as a whole- her flaws, her insecurities, her fears, then I don't think he even loves her." He smiled.

Naina walked a little away from Vivaan. She unbuttons her satin black shirt and the black denim jeans she was wearing, revealing her half naked body.

"Vivaan, how can you love a body like this?" Naina said, as Vivaan saw bruises and scars all over her body. There were few bruises which were still not completely healed, they had turned black. There were scars over her stomach, thighs, and arms, cuts as if she has been cut by a knife all over these places. Another scar was over her chest it was in the shape of circle. There were imprints of belt marks, and a few bruise marks over her chest and shoulders.

Vivaan looked at her and walked to her. He caressed her hair as tears fell from her eyes. Vivaan leaned closer to her and kissed her tears.

"I'm so sorry you had to go through all of this. But Naina, you are a survivor. And a survivor has scars." Vivaan said.

Naina didn't know what to say. Vivaan held her close to his chest as she cried her heart open. Vivaan kissed her tears and everywhere she had her scars. Vivaan made love to those scars and her insecurities and set them all free. Vivaan touched her in such captivating ways even she could never imagine of.

Behind every inch of her skin, Naina felt a soul dying to live.

~

"Would you be able to love her? It wouldn't be easy, Vivaan." Vivaan's mother confessed after Vivaan told her about Naina's past. It was early in the morning, and Naina was still asleep.

"When you choose to love someone who is damaged, you not only take on the weight of their past and pain but also pledge to help them recover from it by being strong and patient." Vivaan replied.

"You know Vivaan, I'm so proud to be your mother."

"And, I'm proud that you gave me such teachings and upbringing." Vivaan smiled.

Vivaan's mother was so awestruck that she couldn't speak anything.

"Naina is a great girl."

"Yes, she is." Vivaan smiled.

Vivaan and her mother were very happy. It looked like after so many years, they were genuinely happy and their family was complete.

"I'll just go and check whether Naina's awake or still sleeping." Vivaan smiled.

"Okay." Vivaan's mother smiled again.

Vivaan walked back into the room to find the woman he loved asleep. He went back to the bed and he sat beside Naina just to adore her sleeping. But she woke up.

"Good Morning." Vivaan smiled and kissed her forehead.

"…Morning." Naina yawned and opened her eyes to find Vivaan looking at her.

Vivaan giggled and said, "Last night was amazing."

Naina blushed.

"You look so beautiful when you blush." Vivaan smiled.

Naina didn't say anything but continued to smile. She hugged Vivaan tightly as she could smell his perfume. She loved such feeling. She felt safe.

"You know I want to have such mornings when we kiss and just cuddle like this for an hour before we say a single word." Vivaan whispered in Naina's ears.

"Shh." Naina said and blushed.

"Don't you shh me." Vivaan laughed and tickled Naina.

Naina laughed. "No! Vivaan!"

Vivaan tickled her more as Naina got up from her bed and ran away from Vivaan.

"You know, I'll catch you, right?" Vivaan laughed evilly.

"You can't!" Naina laughed back.

Vivaan chases Naina and finally grabbed her wrist and pulled her towards him and she fell on his shoulders. Vivaan kisses Naina's forehead.

"I love you." Vivaan smiled.

"I love you so much." Naina smiled back.

"You did not give me my answer." Vivaan said.

"Which?" Naina giggled.

"Oh, you know!"

"No, I don't." Naina laughed.

"Would you like to be Naina Juneja?" Vivaan smiled.

Naina lost her smile somewhere. Vivaan noticed it.

"What happened?" Vivaan asked.

"Vivaan, I…"

"Is it something I said, that offended you?"

"No, not at all, it's just..."

"Yes?" Vivaan caressed her face with his hands and Naina felt so relaxed as if his one-touch set her soul free.

"I'm already legally married, how can I…" Naina said.

Vivaan frowned.

"What will we do now?"

Vivaan didn't respond but kept looking at Naina.

Naina looked at him, "Vivaan."

"Naina,"

"What happened?"

"Nothing, I lost my words looking at your eyes." Vivaan smiled and kissed her forehead.

Naina blushed.

"I know what we will do."

"What?" Naina asked out of curiosity.

"Do you trust me?"

"I trust you more than I trust myself."

"We're going to Reyaansh." Vivaan said.

CHAPTER-28

"Are you crazy?" Naina screamed.

"Naina." Vivaan tried to calm her down.

"No, Vivaan. How can you even think of going to him?"

"Naina, you trust me right?"

"I do, but."

"Then trust me on this, Naina."

"I trust you but I'm scared Vivaan."

"Of what, Naina? Of Reyaansh?"

"I'm afraid that he'll take you away from me like he killed my family away."

Vivaan hugged Naina tightly.

"Oh, Naina!" Vivaan squeezed her tight.

"I love you so much. I promise you nothing will ever happen and nothing can ever keep us apart." Vivaan said.

Naina rested her head on his shoulders. She opened her mouth to say something when suddenly the doorbell rings.

Who are you? What do you want? Wait, with that permission are you getting inside my house?

"Nidhi," The voice said.

Chills ran down her spine. Naina recognized the voice.

Vivaan walked out of the room when suddenly Naina grabbed his hands.

"Don't... Don't go." Naina stammered.

Vivaan gave her a shocking look.

"It's Reyaansh." Naina stammered again.

"How do you know?"

"The voice,"

"You don't have to be scared. You have me, okay?"

Naina held his hands tightly and walked behind Vivaan, to witness Reyaansh standing with some other people.

Reyaansh still looked the same, like he did before. He had the same arrogance and furiousness in his eyes like of a devil with his wicked evil smile.

"Baby," Reyaansh said when he looked at Naina.

Naina tightened the grip on Vivaan's hand.

Reyaansh walked towards her, "I've been searching for you everywhere. I finally found you!" He grabbed Naina's other hand.

"Leave her hand." Vivaan said.

"Oh. Vivaan, I totally forgot about you." Reyaansh said.

"Inspector, please arrest him. He's Vivaan Juneja." Reyaansh said.

Vivaan's mother asked worryingly, "Arrest? With what charges?"

"He has kidnapped Mr. Reyaansh Singhania's wife, Naina Arti Singhania and has forcefully kept her here with him. We have an arrest warrant against him." The inspector said.

"No! No, Vivaan has not kidnapped me." Naina said.

"Right now we have the warrant against him so he has to come with us, we can discuss at the police station." Inspector said.

"I won't let you take him away; you got the warrant for something my son has not even done."

"I'm sorry he has to come with us, with or without your will."

"Mom, Don't worry everything will be okay." Vivaan said.

"I'll come with a lawyer don't you worry okay?"

"Okay." Vivaan said.

They all reached the police station in an hour. Even Vivaan's mother reached at the same time with a lawyer.

"So, what's the matter?" the inspector asked.

"What is the matter? I already told you this guy kidnapped my wife!" Reyaansh said.

"I did not kidnap her!" Vivaan shouted.

"Wait for you two. Let Mrs. Singhania speak." Inspector said.

The words Mrs. Singhania hit Naina so hard as if someone just tried to stab her.

"I… I…" Naina stammered. Reyaansh was staring at her.

"You see, my wife has etiquettes of not speaking against her husband."

Vivaan stretched his arms and grabbed Naina's hands. Naina looked at him and Vivaan was already looking. He smiled and nodded as if he was saying that she doesn't have to be scared of anyone. It gave Naina strength.

"Reyaansh is my husband." Naina said looking at the inspector. "But he never treated me as his wife. He used to hit me, slap me. He ill-treated me. So I ran away." Naina sighed. "Vivaan is someone who helped me come out of my trauma." Naina completed.

"What the hell are you saying?" Reyaansh shouted.

"You keep your voice low, its police station not your house." Inspector shouted.

The lawyer brings some papers and talks to the inspector.

"You can go. All of you." Inspector said.

"Wait-what?" Reyaansh shouted.

"No. We would like to file a complaint against Reyaansh Singhania for doing domestic violence on his wife." Vivaan said.

Everyone looked at Vivaan.

Reyaansh started to laugh. "Oh, this game's gonna be fun to play, Vivaan. You better watch out now." He completed and left.

"I don't want to be his wife anymore. Can I apply for divorce as well?" Naina said.

"Yes you can but you need evidence to prove your allegations against Reyaansh, and I bet you will be leading Mrs. Singhania's case?" The inspector said pointing out to Vivaan.

"Yes." Vivaan said.

"Well, Mr. Juneja all the best! I always respected you for your profession and today, my respect to you multiplied." Inspector smiled.

Vivaan smiled and nodded.

"I'm Kartik Verma, by the way. Senior Inspector of this branch." He introduced himself.

"Nice to meet you, she's Naina." Vivaan said introducing Naina to the inspector.

"Naina?"

"I actually changed my name when I came here so that Reyaansh don't…" Naina choked.

"I got it. Don't worry Mrs. Singhania, you'll have my complete support in this case. If there's any problem do tell me." Kartik said.

"Just, Naina," Naina said.

"Naina, if you anyhow think he can cause any kind of danger to your life or to your loved ones, we can put orders against Reyaansh so he cannot come around you or your loved ones till the final order are passed." The inspector said.

A flashback of what happened to her family sent chills down her spine. She thought if Reyaansh could kill her mother and grandmother then it would be a cakewalk to kill Vivaan, his mother, and Sharara.

"Please-Please, I want that order passed." Naina said.

"Okay, I'll do it. You don't have to be worried anymore."

"When will the proceedings start?" Vivaan asked.

"I'll make sure you get the dates of tomorrow." Kartik said.

"What about the application form?" Vivaan asked.

"Oh, yes! Thanks for reminding."

The inspector gave the application form to Naina and asked her whether she can fill it on her own or would like the inspector to fill it for her. Naina asked the inspector to fill it. Vivaan himself was a lawyer for domestic violence. They all talked and filled the form and they were ensured everything will be fine and they don't have to be worried anymore. *Just like the morning rays takes over the darkness of the world, similarly, someone must step forward to stop and take over the demons walking behind masks of a human. Sometimes God sends his angels to do the work, sometimes god himself has to come to defeat the demons.* Naina couldn't understand who Vivaan was, angel or God?

CHAPTER-29

"I'm so scared. What if we lose? He will take me away." Naina said.

It was evening and Vivaan got all the documents about the case. It said that the first case proceedings will be at 10 am. Everyone was at Vivaan's house, resting on the couch since they had a quite long and hard day.

Kanchan laughed really hard. Naina raised her eyebrows.

"He cannot be defeated; he's the top domestic violence lawyer in Delhi, Naina." Kanchan giggled.

"You trust me, right?" Vivaan said looking at Naina.

"I do."

"Then trust me. I won't let anyone take you away from me." Vivaan caressed her cheeks.

"I love you."

"I love you." Vivaan kissed Naina's forehead.

"Where will we get evidence?" Kanchan asked.

"I don't know." Naina said.

Suddenly Naina's phone ringed.

"Hello?" Naina said, answering the call.

"H-hello?" the voice said.

"Zoya?"

"Nidhi listen to me. I don't have much time. I need to tell you something."

"Zoya where are you? Every time I try the number it's always out of reach. Are you ok?" Naina said.

"Listen to me, Nidhi. I know you're fighting a case against Vivaan."

"How do you know?"

"It doesn't matter. What matters is you need evidence."

"Will you come…" Naina choked.

"Reyaansh's first wife will."

"Wha-What?"

"Rishika Singhania was his first wife and…" before she could say something, the phone got disconnected.

"Hello? Hello? Hello Zoya." Naina said.

"What happened?" Vivaan asked.

"Who's Rishika Singhania?" Naina asked.

"Well I don't know the most of it but, I've heard a lot about her case." Vivaan told.

Vivaan continued, "One of my friends was in this case and he wanted help, so he came to me occasionally while the proceedings took place. The case was hard to win, domestic violence charges against the husband. The lady was all alone fighting, guessing she was an orphan maybe. The case took years in the court as whatever evidence they presented in the court, they were astonishingly proved wrong by the husband. I don't really remember if they did win the case or not." Everyone looked at him as if he were telling a story and they were listening with due interest.

"What happened, Naina?" Vivaan asked.

"She's Reyaansh's first wife." Naina said.

"Unbelievable." Kanchan said.

"He's been married before?" Vivaan asked.

"Zoya told."

"It was Zoya's call?" Vivaan asked.

"Yes. I called back; the phone was out of reach again. I'm so concerned about her whereabouts. I don't know what on earth Reyaansh must've done to her after I left. " Naina said, her eyes were wet. Vivaan walked to her and stretched his arms to hold her. He caressed her back to calm her down.

"We need Rishika to give her testimonial against Reyaansh. And it'll be a win-win case!" Kanchan said.

Naina nodded.

"I'll just give some phone calls and get her present address or phone number." Vivaan said.

Everyone agreed. In the meantime, Kanchan said that she'll help with making the dinner as the cook was on leave. Vivaan's mother agreed and Sharara's caretaker joined them as well. Naina and Sharara talked to each-other while Sharara tried to comfort her. Sharara was small, yet she was matured enough as if she's already 20-30year old.

"We love you, you know that right?" Sharara said.

Naina nodded and gave a faint smile.

"Then trust us, we won't let him run away with things he did wrong." Sharara smiled.

Naina smiled and said, "You are so kind."

"*In a world full of hate, rage, and heartbreaks, someone has to be kind, forgiving and loving to restore the balance.*" Sharara smiled back.

CHAPTER-30

(DAY 1 OF COURT HEARING)

The courtroom was just like how you watch movies or on TV. It was a hall, with the table behind which the judge- who shall decide whether the person is guilty or not by understanding the situation based on testimonials and evidence. Then there was a figure of a lady, with her eyes blindfolded, it was the lady of justice. It means that she will not see a person's wealth or power; she's blind to all differences. That she serves justice without being bias.

Then the court was divided into the sides of the people supporting the two parties with their lawyers. That's where Naina and Reyaansh were, with their lawyers. Reyaansh looked at Naina with hate and such immense rage as if he were set free; he would kill her for filing a police complaint. The media was all over the place but strictly controlled by the police department. Reyaansh Industries were very well known, thus when the complaint was launched against Reyaansh for Domestic Violence, it was a hot topic for everyone to talk about, especially since Vivaan was fighting the case.

The judge arrived and the hearings started. Vivaan walked towards the judge, and then to the audience who were there as a support to both sides. "Domestic violence, we heard this term so many times. We already know about it. It's when the man thinks it's his right to hit a woman because she's his wife and it makes him a

225

man. It's when hitting and beating starts with sometimes to occasionally to monthly and then weekly and then out of a habit, the man starts to beat his wife every day. I wonder where this misconception started."

Vivaan then looked at Reyaansh and raised his voice, "How does hitting a woman make you a man? How can when you reflect pain, scars, and bruises on her body, it'll make you a man? Well, for the starters, it doesn't make you a man it makes you a coward. Not only a coward, it makes you a bastard who beats his own wife for his entertainment in front of the society. And for whom we do not hold any respect." Anger flushed in Vivaan's eyes.

"Mr. Juneja, don't use disrespectful words." The judge said.

"I'm sorry, your honor. As I was saying, we already know what Domestic Violence is. We have already heard what Domestic Violence is." Vivaan turned towards the judge and continued, "We give all our sympathies to the victims of Domestic violence but, I want to ask what do we do to stop it? Domestic Violence is like an uncured disease that is spreading out in the world and we are doing nothing about it because it's rare that the victim gets the justice."

Vivaan took a deep breath and continued, "My lord, women are not like men. They're different. They are much powerful and strong. They were designed with the huge power of tolerance and endurance but that doesn't mean we test her and take her for granted and torture her. I believe in our system, I believe that our victim- Mrs. Nidhi Singhania…" Vivaan choked and turned around to look straight into Naina's eyes and continues, "…will get justice."

"Thank you for enlightening us, Mr. Juneja. Lawyers from Mr. Reyaansh, mind to add your comments on this?" The judge said. All eyes were now on Wasim Khan- the lawyer who was fighting Reyaansh's case.

"Your honor, as we know, Reyaansh Singhania, owner of Singhania Industries, he is a very rich and successful man. He has always been a hardworking man and tried to build high standards for the industries just like his father. But all this money, success, fame, he was not caught up in it. He's a very down to the earth person. Kind and generous are the two adjectives which would suit the best for him. Ever since their parents died and his brother, Rehmaan, Reyaansh being an adopted child not only took care of the company single-handedly but also took care of the sister, Zoya Singhania like a father providing her the best luxury, best education. In his company, he treats his employees just like his family. For which I've provided written testimonials from every worker in the company who has ever worked with or for Reyaansh proving his good character. He has also done charity works for many orphanages and one of them is St. Mary Orphanage, from where he was adopted since he never forgot the people who took him into their wings and gave him shelter and love even before the Singhania's did. The charity work also extended to divorced women and victimized women welfare organizations and he made sure time to time that they do not face any kind of problems in the world alone. He dealt with their problems personally, and if any legal issues were there, Reyaansh made sure I was involved." Wasim took a deep breath and turned towards the judge.

"A man with such good records, how can he ill-treat his wife when all he has been giving is love, in his till life? I

227

can say without a hesitation that my client is being framed for the things he never did nor can he think of doing, ever." Wasim ended.

"Hearing both sides, the court is now adjourned till the next hearing which shall be held the day after tomorrow, at 10 am. We shall go through the evidence and testimonials." The judge said and walked out of the courtroom.

Naina looked at Vivaan and smiled. Vivaan held her hands and smiled back and walked out the courtroom. Wasim and Reyaansh were standing in front of their cars as if they were waiting for them to come.

"Vivaan, my dear friend!" Wasim said.

"Wasim," Vivaan looked at Naina and gestured him to leave. She refrained but Vivaan insisted, so she agreed.

"That was one heck of a speech on domestic violence; I must say I'm moved." Wasim grinned while Reyaansh laughed.

"Oh, you liked it? Wait till you hear my winning speech. You'll be the blown off your feet." Vivaan smiled.

"One should be confident, Vivaan. Over-confidence kills." Wasim said.

"Repeat this sentence twice a day and I bet you'll be good to go, my friend." Vivaan laughed.

"Vivaan, Vivaan, Vivaan." Reyaansh walked towards them.

"How's Sharara? That girl you brought home, rescuing? Being a hero, huh? And I remember I met her last night, I saw her; she's all grown up now. A woman, a beautiful one indeed…" Reyaansh said when Vivaan interrupted and walked close to Reyaansh holding his collars, "Keep your eyes off, from Sharara you understand? You better do."

The police sensed a disputed and rushed towards Vivaan and Reyaansh.

"What's going on here?" The inspector said.

"Nothing, this man was just leaving to search for his little friend. He just told she's been missing." Reyaansh said leaving Vivaan scared and speechless.

~

"Call me as soon as you find Sharara." Vivaan said to the caretaker as they rushed back to their house. They brought Sharara back from the rehabilitation center today in the morning concerning her safety.

"Tell me what happened, Vivaan?" Naina asked looking at Vivaan.

Vivaan doesn't utter a word. Naina kept trying to talk to him but he does not say a word. When their car arrived at Vivaan's home, he rushed out the car to find Sharara inside her room, playing.

"Where were you, Oh dear lord you scared me!" Vivaan exclaimed.

"I'm sorry, I was in the garden playing when a little girl came saying her friend knows you and he's with you so he left that girl here, for I to take care. She wanted to have an ice cream and she had money and I went with her." Sharara said.

"Don't ever do that okay?"

"The girl still was a stranger, and what have I told you about strangers?"

"To not to talk to them or go anywhere with them,"

"So remember that, okay?"

"Okay." Sharara said.

Vivaan kissed her forehead and left. Naina stood there and was watching everything from a distance. She was in awe of him yet was concerned; she couldn't understand what exactly was going on his mind. Naina followed him as he walked back into his room. His room was slightly dark, yet was lit with the sunlight that escaped from the windows.

Vivaan sat on the bed, Naina was about to switch on the lights. Vivaan looked up and gestured her not to. Naina walked to him and sat beside him.

"Vivaan,"

"Naina,"

"Talk to me. Tell me what happened?"

"Reyaansh…" Vivaan choked.

Naina looked at him continuously waiting for his further response.

"Reyaansh threatened me. And today Sharara wasn't mysteriously disappeared, that little girl Sharara talked about was sent by Reyaansh. As if, he's giving me threats that he'll do something so wrong, he went to see Sharara in the rehab yesterday as well and the way he told about Sharara to me, I…" Vivaan's voice broke.

"Hey, shh," Naina hugged him.

Vivaan held her tightly.

"Vivaan, I love you. I've always known I did love you but this fear, maybe the fear of love was so over-powering that I never dared to accept it. You know, you are that one person who taught me one mustn't fear love; it is like strength, to behold. You are my strength and will always be my strength. But Vivaan, I want you to be safe. I want your loved ones to be safe as well. So if you want to run for the hills, I'm with you. Let's just go somewhere, a place where there's no fear of love, but the beauty of it is cherished. Let's run away from this harsh reality, to build our own world of fiction."

"Naina,"

"Vivaan,"

"Naina, I love you. And that is why; I will fight for you and the self-respect you lost. I'm going to fight for you so that whenever you look into the mirror, you don't feel defeated. I'm not quitting. I'll never quit. It's you, and I'll always fight for you, no matter if I've to fight the whole damn world. I'll keep you safe, I'll keep us safe. We will build a home, darling, a home that would be more beautiful than fiction and as close to reality."

"Oh, Vivaan," Naina sobbed while she hugged Vivaan. She also knew he was crying. Naina made him lie down and he kept his head on her lap. She caressed his head; she was running her fingers through his silky soft hairs. She parted her whole hair on the right side and leaned to kiss his forehead. She wiped his tears, as she calmed him down. And within a fraction of a minute, he slept like a baby. *And Naina looked at the man she loved, the man who protects her like a warrior protects his family, giving up everything and not fearing the unknown.*

~

It was evening when Vivaan tried his level best to get in contacts with either Reyaansh's first wife- Rishika or Zoya. He called his friend, the lawyer who fought Rishika's case but his number was out of reach. He kept on dialing different numbers. He tried to get new leads, only to get a dead end.

"We are trying to find evidence in a wrong place." Vivaan said.

"What do you mean?" Naina said.

"We need to go back to the place where it all started." Vivaan said.

"Oh, so you are suggesting that we should go…" Kanchan couldn't finish when Naina cut her in.

"No! No, not at all," Naina said anxiously.

"We must, we only have a day and if we want to win, we need to leave. In fact, we must leave today so that we can search evidence tomorrow." Vivaan said.

Naina sighs.

"Get your bags packed Naina; we're going to start from the beginning." Vivaan said.

"Dehradun, it is then." Naina said in a small voice.

CHAPTER-31

The house which once was the place- a place where Naina was brought up, was given life lessons and a place where she understood love, was turned was ruins and black ashes; from the little garden to the house inside. Nothing had left. Every possibility of life in the place was no more, which was on the contrary to the beautiful morning in Dehradun. The wind blew while the birds chirped; everything seemed to be perfect but Naina's life.

"I came back…" Naina choked and looked at Vivaan, she continued, "I came back before leaving Delhi."

Vivaan stretched his hands to hold hers, little did he knew that nothing could ever comfort her when she thought of that horrifying memory when her own house was being burned down in front of her eyes and she couldn't do a thing but to scream in pain and cry her lungs out, to feel helpless.

"It was too late." Tears flushed down her cheeks.

"…I don't even know where their bodies are, whether their bodies survived or…" She said in a small voice controlling her best to not to cry.

The thing, about pain, is no matter how hard we try, we can never move on from that one thing which hurt us so bad that we shiver even at the thought of it. It gives us chills at the night, haunting us, making us hard to

233

breathe. Alas, it doesn't leave us in the day either. It latches itself upon us like a demon. And, the only way out of it is to learn how to distract self from those thoughts. Some learn how to shift thoughts, some let those thoughts live among themselves.

"He'll pay for every wrong he has ever done to you, and your family, Naina. But I need your help. We have only 1 day, to get him behind the bars, to make him pay for his deeds, Naina..." Vivaan stopped and looked at her, "...To avenge your dead family, Naina." He said.

Naina looked at him and wiped her tears.

You are going to wish that you were dead instead, Reyaansh Singhania. I'm coming after you. Naina thought to herself.

~

"Maya, please help us. Just come. Support the truth, Maya. Please." Naina Requested.

Naina was in the office where she once worked, a place where it all started; where she went to start working with Reyaansh, and where everything started to come crashing down, not instantly yet, slowly. Naina and Vivaan decided to try to get some evidence, any evidence against Reyaansh so that they could use it against him. And, there were two places where they could find the best evidence- Reyaansh's home and office. Vivaan made sure, Reyaansh wasn't in Dehradun, and ironically he was in Delhi while Naina and Vivaan were in his office looking for evidence against him. According to the plan, they had decided that Naina will try convincing the office employees she once knew to help them, to give statements against Reyaansh if not then to keep them occupied while Vivaan searched the CCTV footage.

"I know what happened to you and your family, Nidhi. After knowing and suffering everything, how can you even think of coming to me and to ask me for helping you? Are you insane?" Maya exclaimed in a high pitch which was more scared.

"It happened to me, Maya. It could've happened to you or any other employee. What would you do then?"

"Well it didn't happen to me, as a matter of fact, I warned you. Still, you chose to enter the lion's den." Maya said.

"He used to beat me, not once a month or week, every day! Sometimes twice-thrice a day, he burned the palm of my head with the stove, he used to keep me locked in the house; he killed my mother and my grandmother for heaven's sake, Maya, please!" Naina took a deep breath reminding herself of not to feel weak, "Help me get that bastard." She completed.

"I'm sorry. I'll pass." Maya said with pity in her voice.

"I wish, Maya, with the deepest of my heart, that if he walks out from this free again, you don't end up as his next prey." Naina said. She started to walk away when Maya stopped her.

"You said again, did you know that he was once married before you?" Maya asked in surprise.

"I found out recently."

"When I say this, do not react, Reyaansh watches the CCTV footage and he can easily tell when something is fishy, just reading someone's expression. Just look at me and pretend you're shouting or something." Maya said.

"OKAY!" Naina pretended.

"His ex-wife, she's dead. She died at the last court hearing, while her way back to home. She had successfully won her case but she couldn't even make out a day alive." Maya said.

Naina couldn't understand. Zoya said Rishika can help with the case if had she died, she definitely wouldn't say such things. Maybe there's some another clue to this. Naina thought to herself.

"I can give you her address, you want it?" Maya said.

Naina nodded. Maya gave her the address to an old building apartment located in a quiet place on the outskirts of Dehradun.

"Take care, Nidhi. May God be with you," Maya gave her a faint smile. This time she looks up in the CCTV while smiling. Naina feels odd.

"Naina?" Vivaan arrived suddenly, "We need to go." He said.

"Did you get it?" Naina asked.

"More than you can ask for." Vivaan gave her a victorious smile.

"What about you?" Vivaan asked Naina.

"More than you can ask for." Naina smiled back.

~

"Do you believe in ghosts?" Vivaan asked as he got out of the car.

"No." Naina gave him a weird look.

"Well, we'd need Rishika's ghost to talk to us, to tell us everything." Vivaan laughed.

"It's not funny Vivaan." Naina said.

"Well it is, I already told you, I have CCTV footage against Reyaansh. So why are we here? We can go back to Delhi and celebrate our victory on the case tomorrow, my love!" Vivaan broadens his smile as he wraps his arms around her neck. Naina shoves his arms away. Naina saw 'Mehra's' written on the nameplate, even when the apartment number was right. She guessed it must be her house before she became a 'Singhania'.

"Zoya told us about Rishika. There has to be something. There needs to be something. I mean, if it was a dead end, then why would Zoya call us and tell us about this, anyway?" Naina said and walked into the apartment.

The apartment was dark as the lights were off. It was slightly cleaned and well organized. It looked as if someone had lived here recently or still was living here. Naina went inside, Vivaan followed her. Naina started looking for clues or evidence or anything which could tell her why Zoya led her to a dead end or to Rishika. She went through books to files to drawers to the bedroom to closets to cupboards, to study tables. She saw a laptop; she picked it up and walked outside the bedroom, to see Vivaan sitting on the couch using his phone.

"Vivaan!" Naina said furiously.

"Oh god, you scared me, Naina! What?" Vivaan looked at her surprisingly.

"We were supposed to look out for clues and you are using your phone and resting on the couch? What happened to- you need to take avenge on your family Naina or I love you and I'll be there for you to support you!" Naina shouted.

Vivaan got up and walked to her. He caressed her cheek she shoved it away, he did it again until she allowed him to caress her and comfort her, to calm her.

"I was sending the CCTV video to the inspector, to my mother and saving it on other places, to keep the evidence safe for just in case, you know."

"Oh." Naina said.

Vivaan brought his forehead close to Naina's and rested it as he held her by the back of her neck.

"I'm sorry, for shouting at you." Naina said.

"It's okay! Let's see what you got there." Vivaan said taking the laptop from Naina's hand.

Vivaan and Naina sat on the couch and opened the laptop. Luckily it was not password-protected. They opened up to see a picture of Rishika, black hair, chubby cheeks with black eyes. She was wearing very light lipstick that matched her skin-tone, with smoky eye makeup. She was beautiful but the picture or Rishika was with another man, with brown hair who looked Irish.

"Wow." Vivaan said.

"Yeah, wow. Let's try to focus on how to collect her information now, shall we?" Naina said and Vivaan nodded.

There were many pictures of Rishika and the Irish man on the laptop; they guessed the Irish guy as Rishika's boyfriend. But what turned tables were when they saw wedding pictures of Rishika with the same Irish man.

"If that is Rishika…" Naina looked palely at Vivaan.

"We are being framed we need to get out right now." Vivaan said holding Naina's hand and as soon as he got up, someone entered the apartments. It was quite dark but it was visible that he had a gun.

He walked ahead, and he wasn't alone. He switched on the light to reveal who he was. It was Reyaansh, with Zoya whose hands were all tied up with rope and her mouth covered with tape. Reyaansh was smiling.

"Leaving so early?" Reyaansh said pointing out his gun.

Vivaan and Naina stopped.

"The party's getting all started now."

CHAPTER-32

"You literally thought you're winning?" Reyaansh laughed.

Vivaan and Naina didn't say a word as they sat on the couch while Reyaansh was sitting on the table next to them. Naina felt like she was back in her days where Reyaansh was always a step ahead of her.

Reyaansh laughed.

"You fly to Dehradun- my city and you think I wouldn't know? Wait, you thought Zoya led you here?" He laughed again.

"This little bitch who betrayed his own brother who wished nothing but good for her from all his heart, who never touched her let alone beat her, you thought she's better than me?" Reyaansh paused, "YOU THOUGHT SHE'S BETTER THAN ME? YOU THOUGHT SHE'D GET AWAY FROM WHAT SHE DID TO ME?" Reyaansh shouted.

Reyaansh took a deep breath as he scratched his cheek. "You know what? Open her tape and rope."

Naina looked at Reyaansh.

"DO AS I SAY!" He placed his gun on Naina's forehead now.

Naina and Vivaan untied the ropes and removed the tape from Zoya's face. Tears burst out from Zoya's eyes.

"I'm so sorry Nidhi! He said he's kidnapped someone you love, and if I don't agree to call you, he'll the little girl." Zoya cried.

"Who? Sharara?" Naina cried. Reyaansh placed the gun on the back of her head.

"Do you know why I kept you alive all along? Because I thought you know where Nidhi is. But now that I have her, you can join the others who have betrayed me. Hope you will choose to be on my side in your next life." Reyaansh said.

"Reyaansh please don't kill h…" Before Naina could say anything, Reyaansh fired the gun, resulting Zoya's blood spilled all over Naina's face and hands.

Naina screamed out loud. Taking an advantage of Reyaansh's distraction, Vivaan kicked Reyaansh so hard that the gun fell down from his hands.

"I TOLD YOU TO STAY AWAY FROM SHARARA!" Vivaan shouted at Reyaansh as he kicked him hard with his feet. He bent and grabbed him to beat him again. Within a fraction of a minute, Reyaansh took control and started beating Vivaan, hard and threw him on the kitchen shelf. And then, he stabbed Vivaan's back with a chef's knife. He then hit his head with a vase. Vivaan fell down on the floor with his blood spilling out; as he slowly loses his conscience and everything slowly fades, he hears another gunshot.

EPILOGUE

"According to a folk tale, Chandrama (Moon) had many wives but he loved Rohini the most. Alas, Rohini and Chandrama lived far away from each other. He could meet her only once in a month. Some say it's Chandrama's unconditional love to Rohini that even after so many obstacles, he never give up on her and comes every month to her. Just to meet Rohini. But some say, it's he's helplessness. He has to come every month to meet her and he can't do anything about it because they both are connected." Vivaan sighed.

"Naina, see I've started to talk like you." Vivaan smiled with a heavy heart.

"What kind of a love do you have for me from those two options?" Naina smiled.

Naina wore a red saree just like she wore on the day she met Vivaan.

"I'm helpless Naina, to be honest. Yes, I'm helpless because I need you. I need you for me. I need you when I wake up to see your face as the first thing in the morning. I need you when I'm sad for you to hug me tight and to tell me that everything will be okay. I need you for you to love me in my loneliest nights. I need you. I want you. It's okay I think love can make you selfish sometimes." Vivaan said.

"Oh, Vivaan," Naina caressed his cheeks and smiled.

"But Naina, I'm in love with you." Vivaan looked at Naina and smiled.

Naina smiled, "I love you so much."

"So much,"

"I'll always be with you, Vivaan." Naina said.

"Vivaan, what are you doing in the garden?" The nurse asked.

Vivaan looked at the nurse.

"Have you been hallucinating again, dear?" The nurse asked.

Suddenly when Vivaan looked around at Naina, She was not there, but a grave.

Tears fell from Vivaan's eyes, "Why?" he thought to himself.

He looked at the nurse. "You scared her. You made her go away from me, why did you do this?"

"Vivaan," The nurse said.

"Why!" Vivaan screamed out loud.

"You know better, Vivaan. What happened that evening, you know better." said the nurse quietly.

Vivaan closed his eyes and wiped his tears. Reality chilled his heart and his Naina was fiery flames on ice.

The nurse took him back to the car, Vivaan sat down near the window. As the car started, Vivaan walked down to the harsh memory lane. The evening when everything changed and his life took a devastating turn.

Vivaan was lost in his ever-going thoughts, when the nurse said, "We have reached."

"I can go on my own." Vivaan said and walked out of the car.

He walked to his room. His room was dark.

"You're back? I missed you." Naina said.

"I still miss you." Vivaan said.

"Did you enjoy your day today?"

"No."

Suddenly the nurse turns on the lights of the room, and says, "Who are you talking to?"

Vivaan looks at Naina to find her gone.

"It's okay." The nurse said.

The old lady hugged Vivaan and put him to the bed. "Try to get some sleep okay?" she said.

"Naina was here." Vivaan whispered.

"Naina is no more, Vivaan."

The words sent chills down his spine.

"I'm sorry." The nurse said and walked out of the room turning off the light.

The gunshot killed Naina on one go. Reyaansh hit Naina for one last time, taking her breaths away forever as he shot her in her heart. There was no time to say a final goodbye or to exchange 'I love you' as well. The police arrested Reyaansh as being guilty the next day when he was trying to escape from the country.

Vivaan wanted to take her to the hospital but the doctors said it was too late and apologized for his loss, and Vivaan lost everything that day; not only Naina but also his senses. He was so traumatized. He closed his eyes and the glimpse from the graveyard appeared on his mind.

'Those we love don't go away; they walk beside us every day. -Naina Arti Juneja' was written on the top of the grave on the headstone.

He opened his eyes out of fear; he walked out of the bed to the drawer and grabbed a box.

The box was old and was made up of wood. He opened it. There was a blue box and a letter. He opened the letter which said:

"Vivaan,

Loving a person from a distance is easy; staying in a relationship maintaining it is harder. There will be times when you'll get angry at me when I'll get angry at you. There will be times when all the things we planned wouldn't work out and there will be a time when you'll think, is it right? Is it really what I wanted?

Love isn't easy, especially when you're in love with a person who is too broken and cares too much. But, Vivaan I want to have this journey with you. I want you to know that no matter what. I'm willing to walk in this life with you, only with you because I'm in love with you.

You can't say what the future brings to us, but whatever it brings I want to tell you that you won't be alone facing it. I will be with you. You asked me to marry you twice, today Vivaan. I'll ask you. Tomorrow after winning the case, will you marry me? I am bad at proposing. But I did bring a ring. They say that engagement ring is worn on the right hand's finger because there's a vein that is connected to the heart. You said people meet for a reason, it wasn't a cliché. You met me, to breathe me back to life.

Wear this ring, and I'll always be with you. I love you so much.

Naina."

Reading this letter Vivaan looked at his right-hand finger and he was wearing the metallic silver ring and his fingers clasped into Naina's hands. Tears fell from his eyes to their hands.

"You left me after pulling me towards yourself like a moon pulls the sea, you just left, without warnings. Why, Naina?"

"I'm here Vivaan. I'll always be here with you." Naina said.

"I need you with me, come back."

"Our love has transcended time, reasons and distance, Vivaan that I can never be convinced that I wasn't destined to be with you. We're meant to be together always and forever, my love. I'll meet you again in a new face, in a new life but with this same heart that loves you intensely, passionately and deeply. I'll always stay with you." Naina caressed his face.

Vivaan sighed deeply.

"But till then, I will stay." Naina smiled.

"You exist by your smile and your presence. You exist in nature. You are part of the sea, and part of the well-nourished plants, you are in this sun, and you are immersed in timelessness. *You're frozen by time*, just for me." Vivaan said.